MARY & THE ALIEN

Mary & the Alien

ASHLEY GOOD

Dedicated to all of the weird kids,
past and present.

You make the world
a more wonderful place.

Chapter One

Thursday, June 12th

It was a warm summer night on June the 12th, 1947. The town of Falkland was silent and ready for bed, as the darkness of night rolled across the sky and blanketed the tiny town. Life was silent, except for the chirping of insects and the faint yet eerie howl of coyotes.

Leaning out of the window of the bedroom that she shared with her brother, Mary closed her eyes and took a deep breath, inhaling the gentle summer air. Dry brittle grass that smelled of straw, crisp pine needles, and the faint but salty smell of that night's dinner filled her nose. She smiled, enjoying this rare moment of quiet reprise.

"What planet is that?"

She looked down at her little brother, George, who was using a cardboard tube as a telescope.

"That bright one? It's called Venus." Mary gently twisted the cardboard tube. "Do you see the one that is kind of orange? That is Mars."

While only nine years old, Mary couldn't remember a time when she wasn't looking after her brother. A cherub-faced four-year-old, George still had a childish sense of wonder, which Mary was determined to protect. She knew that the cardboard tube wasn't a real telescope, she was almost ten years old after all, but Mary was happy for any moment of levity that she could share with her brother.

"Mary, what's the difference between a planet and a star?"

"We haven't gotten that far in school yet."

"I can't wait to go to school like you."

Mary could still recall the day that her mother, Margaret, overspent and bought a roll of paper towel to use in the kitchen. She also remembered her mother's second husband, Friedrich, screaming as he threw a tantrum over the purchase. It was impossible for Mary to understand why he would be so upset over something as silly as a roll of soft paper. They worked better than old kitchen towels, and didn't he want her mother to be happy?

She missed her real dad, who died shortly after George was born. Neither sibling knew much about their father's early life, except that he moved up from the United States when he was young, and could always make them laugh. To Mary it didn't feel as though her mother cared much about losing him though. Margaret pulled back. Went numb. Mary was unable to remember much from this period, only that her mom stopped hugging her. Six months later Margaret married Friedrich, the man that would later scream at her over paper towel. Mary couldn't yet understand the world of adults, she just knew that she wanted to be left out of it for as long as possible.

Mary looked down at George who appeared lost in thought staring through his telescope. Almost as if she had manifested it by thinking about it, the peaceful evening was interrupted by the sounds of Margaret and Friedrich screaming. At first muffled, the sound grew louder and louder as they moved into their bedroom, which shared a wall with Mary and George's.

George looked at Mary knowingly, set his telescope down, and climbed into his unmade bed.

While they had both become skilled at ignoring the yelling, the siblings would never get used to the pounding radiating from the wall of their mother's room. Mary caught a glimpse of the fighting one night when she got up for a glass of water. The bedroom door was cracked open just enough for her to witness Friedrich's scrawny and liver-spotted fist slamming against the wall, just shy of her mother's face. Mary was thirsty this evening as well, but she now knew that things like water and going to the washroom should wait for the morning.

Thud. Thud. Thud.

Each thud made Mary flinch.

"Could you read me a story?"

"Not tonight, Georgie."

It was hard for Mary to say no to her little brother. His big doll eyes always got to her. On nights like this, though, Mary knew it was best for the two of them to just go to sleep. The faster that they went to sleep, the sooner that it would be morning.

Mary grabbed Mr. Purdy, George's faithful companion, off the shelf. Their real father gave the bear to George when he was born. Even if there was no way for George to truly remember something from that age, he must have had some residual idea that this bear was from his father, as it was the only thing that was guaranteed to give him comfort.

George gave Mary a big hug as she passed him the dusty bear.

"Good night, Mary."

"Good night, Georgie."

Mary climbed into her bed. The thuds had stopped, replaced by a woman's sobs. Mary took a small portable radio out from under her pillow. On the back of the radio was a small inscription:

To Mary, Love Dad.

Her dad gifted the radio to her in confidence, when he was ill. *No one's supposed to have these yet, Mary. How neat is that?* She could still hear his voice when she focused. Mary turned the radio on at its lowest volume level and placed her head against it to drown out her mother's sobbing.

Chapter Two

Friday, June 13th

It was one of those hot summer days where all anyone could think about was jumping into a cold lake. Everywhere you went, the ambient noise of grasshoppers clicking and hopping through the dead dry grass was inescapable. The only patches of grass that remained green were the few lucky spots shielded by the thirsty pine trees.

Mary stared longingly out of her classroom window. She took a deep breath, and felt the sweet warm air fill her lungs. Open windows always brought her comfort.

Ms. Susan Webb, voted everyone's favourite elementary school teacher for five years in a row according to the Okanagan Commoner newspaper, wiped the days lessons off the board. The other students rushed to leave the classroom, but Mary remained distracted, and also partially stuck to her sweaty plastic school seat.

"Mary?"

Mary jumped slightly, startled by her teacher.

"You can go home now."

Mary hated hearing those words, but she enjoyed hearing Ms. Webb say them. Ms. Webb had one of those voices that could soothe a mountain lion. She could have announced that the school was under attack by the Axis, and it still would have sounded melodic to Mary's ears.

"Huh? Oh…" Mary looked around at all the empty desks. The gross feeling of shame began to wash over her. She was so embarrassed to waste her teachers time like this. "I'm sorry Miss Webb, I got distracted."

"It's okay, Mary. The heat makes all of us sleepy."

She really did love her teacher. Why couldn't Ms. Webb be her mom? She wouldn't yell and scream at her kids or invite strange men over. Mary couldn't imagine Ms. Webb inviting any mean people over at all. She seemed like a woman who enjoyed her space. Maybe she had a cat? Mary liked to imagine that she did.

Mary gathered up her book bag and began to walk towards the classroom door.

"You know that usually I would let you stay in class a while longer, but I have a meeting with Principal Sanders shortly."

"I… I know…" The dry air caused the words to get stuck in Mary's throat. "I just don't want to go home is all."

Ms. Webb leaned in and gave Mary a hug.

"I understand that things aren't good with your mom and step-dad, but they love you in their own ways."

"I'm not sure that they do, though."

"You're a good kid. Anyone would be so lucky to have you as a daughter!"

Even if those words wouldn't change anything, they still felt good to hear. Ms. Webb handed Mary her book report, which had a big red A written on it, with a little smiley face in the corner.

Book bag strapped to her back, and book report in hand, Mary stepped outside of the school. The sun instantly blinded her, but she didn't mind. Sometimes she welcomed uncomfortable moments, as they offered a moment of reprise from her otherwise repetitive existence. What she didn't welcome, though, was being tripped by the only three people that she hated as much as her stepfather.

Within a matter of seconds, Mary went from standing up right to collapsing onto the sizzling concrete steps of the school.

"Oof! And she's down!"

Mary looked down at her skinned knee. She rubbed the blood off with the palm of her hand and began to pick out the few pieces of grit left behind. Three laughing shadows approached her.

Lucy, Don, and Ricky, were, as far as Mary was concerned, worse than the Devil himself. Their torment was inescapable. No matter what she did, whether it was a good day, or bad, they were always there. Waiting. Lingering. Biding their time until they felt it was the perfect time to strike.

"Aww, poor little Mary. All alone without her lamb. Where's your lamb, Mary?" The lead turkey vulture, Lucy, mocked.

Lucy was the preacher's daughter. How cliché. Her blonde curls reminded Mary of the angels on her school's Christmas tree. She felt guilty for associating a demon like Lucy with such a pretty memory. Mary tucked her long thick brown hair behind her ears and dusted herself off. "That's not even a creative insult."

This time the second member of the flock, Ricky, the skinnier of the two sidekicks, pushed Mary, causing her to fall again. This time Mary stayed on the ground. Lucy walked closer and stood over Mary. "I heard she really did have a lamb, but her folks were so poor that they made her eat it!" The evil Christmas ornament incarnate chirped to her two loyal servants.

"How'd you like mutton, Mary?" The original tripper, Don, mocked. His fat cheeks jiggled as he laughed.

And with that, Mary jumped up and tackled Lucy. Mary's family didn't celebrate Christmas, anyway.

"Cat fight!" Ricky called out, while taking a step back and running his fingers through his wavy black hair.

"Get off of me, you freak!" Lucy yelled with disgust.

Mary took a step back. Her face burned with rage.

"Uh oh, we made her mad now!" Don squawked, hands on his hips like chubby wings.

The three brats hurried away haphazardly with their arms in the air. Even in escape, they found a way to make fun of

Mary. Mary watched them for a bit, hoping to herself that they wouldn't double back. She straightened out her clothes, smoothed the creases from her book report, and began to walk home. She only made it a few feet though before she realized that the three bullies were still watching her.

"That's right, you better get home for dinner!" Lucy taunted. "Baaaaa!"

Mary continued to walk home with her head held high. It was only when she was several blocks away, when she was certain that neither Lucy, Ricky, or Don were watching her, that she brushed the warm salty tears off of her cheeks.

Over an hour and several sweaty miles later, Mary reached her house. Standing at the top of the driveway, she paused for a minute. The house, a single level rancher, was old. Even for 1940s sensibilities. The yard and flower beds were unkempt. A rusty old tire swing hung from the lone dry pine tree in the front yard. She remembered her father hanging it up, during happier times. Now the ground under the swing was littered with equally rusty beer tins.

Abruptly very aware of how poor her family was, she dusted off her clothes once again. She didn't want to be envious of the mean kids at school, but sometimes it was difficult not to be. Looking down at her skinned knee, which had begun to heal and was coated in a thick crimson scab, Mary took a deep breath and walked into the house.

Careful not to make a noise, she opened the screen door as slowly as possible. After years of practice, she could confidently navigate her way through the creaky old house without making a sound. Mary couldn't help but think that she would make a fantastic explorer one day. She knew that she would never fall prey to one of those weird jungle booby traps. With her head down, she set her book bag down on the floor, and carefully removed her shoes. Step by careful step, Mary only managed to creep halfway to her bedroom before she was spotted. Maybe she wouldn't be a great explorer after all...

"Mary Louis Schmidt! Get in here and help me make dinner." Mary's mother, Margaret, barked from the kitchen. Mary could remember a time when her mom's voice was gentler, like Mrs. Webb's. Softer. Kinder. Over the years though, her softness had warn away until all that was left were her hard edges. Mary missed how her mother used to be but knew that part of her died alongside her father.

Mary walked into the kitchen without saying a word. She wanted to tell her Mom about her skinned knee, and be comforted. She kept a straight face though. Mary knew that the best way to stay out of trouble was to stay quiet and kept her chin up. Alert, but not too confident, lest she be seen as smug. Margaret shoved a partially plucked pheasant into Mary's unexpecting hands. "Pluck this. And hurry. Your father's been out all day and we need to have things ready when he gets home."

Mary opened her mouth to rebut the father comment, but knew it was best to stay quiet. She looked at the limp bird carcass. Its feathers wilted and stuck to its body like an old dog that had been left in the rain. The bird's melted feathers gave off an odd smell which made Mary think of the hair salon.

She looked at the ends of her own hair. How it hung over her shoulders like wavy chestnut coloured curtains. Rogue pieces hung down and grazed the pheasant as she plucked it. Her mother's hair was long and dark too but had begun to grey around the corners by her eyes. They both had hazel eyes as well. Mary was very much her mother's daughter.

"I can help, too!" George announced proudly as he waddled into the kitchen wearing a striped shirt and short pants. Although it was unspoken, everyone assumed he must have inherited his cute traits from his father.

"Want to help us, Georgie? Go outside and dig up some of those potatoes." Margaret said with a slight hint of sarcasm.

George nodded, and hurried outside like the good boy he was. There were times Mary couldn't help but be a little envious of him, too. He often escaped the brunt of their parent's wrath. Mary wondered if it was because George looked the most like their dead father. God, she missed him so much. As with her jealousy of the three class bullies, this also made Mary sick with guilt. She found that she was envious of a lot, lately. And the guilt was always quick to follow.

Plucking off the wet feathers sounded a lot like tearing wet newspaper. It reminded Mary of the time she made a paper mâché monster in class. While the sound wasn't innately bothersome, knowing that she was pulling out the feathers that once allowed the bird to fly, to be free, made Mary deeply uncomfortable. She finally decided to speak. "I got an A on my book report, Mama."

"That's good, Mary… But your father and I have been talk-ing."

Mary finished plucking the pheasant and placed its body in the kitchen sink.

"We're not sure if school's right for you anymore. I work my behind off all day and could use your help around the house."

"Why doesn't—" Mary paused in thought for a moment. "*He* help out more."

"You know your father—"

Mary subtly recoiled at the word.

"Goes out during the day."

"Yeah, drinking." Oops. Mary wished she hadn't said that.

"Watch your mouth," Margaret barked. She raised her hand to Mary but didn't follow through with her threat.

"You know that man provides for us. You don't have any idea how hard it is for an older woman with two kids to find a man!" The words fell out of Margaret's mouth, as if she had played them over and over in her head before. "You count your lucky stars that he came into our life."

Suddenly, Margaret and Mary both heard the front door bang open. *Friedrich would make an even worse jungle explorer than me,* Mary thought to herself. *He would definitely set off all of the traps, get shot with an arrow, get kidnapped, and have his head shrank.*

Margaret instantly pivoted towards the fridge and grabbed a bottle of beer for her husband. Mary found it oddly bemusing to see how her mom handled this task. It was the closest thing to ballet that she would ever witness.

Friedrich was a wiry old man. Old enough to be Mary's grandpa, for sure. He was always slightly greasy looking, as if he had been hard at work outside. Mary knew that he didn't work though. No matter how hard her mother worked to keep Friedrich's clothes starched and pressed, he always looked dirty.

Friedrich sauntered into the house and plopped that day's hunting score down on to the kitchen floor. Blood oozed out of the bag, slowly spreading across the vinyl checkerboard. Unconcerned, he began to participate in Margaret's trashy ballet. In one singular motion he leaned his shot gun against the side of the kitchen table with his left hand and took the beer bottle from Margaret with his right, before popping open the top of the beer bottle with his yellowed teeth. A regular prima ballerina.

"You two talk about Mary's classes yet?"

Her patience gone; Mary stomped out of the kitchen.

Later that evening, Mary and her family sat down to eat dinner. Family dinners at the Schmidt-Johnson household were not a formal affair. Each night, regardless of what was said earlier or who yelled at whom, come hell or high water the family would sit together in the living room, eating off trays and listening to the radio. There was never any reconciliation after a fight. Sometimes Mary wasn't sure if her mother and Friedrich could pick up on the tension at dinner time, or if they were ignorant of it. Mary assumed they kept their faces stuffed purposefully so that they wouldn't have to talk to each other. Dinner was never that tasty.

"I don't understand why Prime Minister King wants to start sending our money over to Europe. They got my boy already, isn't that enough?" Friedrich barked through his mouthful of greasy pheasant. He slammed his bottle of beer down, causing the dinner tray to shake and the drink to foam over.

"Boom!" George cheered with a playful giggle.

"War's not funny! Goddamn little brat." Friedrich raised his hand to George. If Mary's mom couldn't feel the tension before, Mary knew that she felt it then. The atmosphere fell still, and everything slowed down as if the room had been filled up with sand.

"Georgie, go to your room," Margaret spoke in her softest tone.

George's eyes welled up with tears., and he quickly ran to his room. Mary could hear the door slam from down the hall.

"Mary, grab a cloth," Margaret ordered.

Mary stood up, instinctively following her mother's orders. But then, she hesitated for a moment. "I'm sick of this. I hate cleaning up all of your messes!"

And with one instantaneous swing, Friedrich slapped her.

The crack of Friedrich's leathery old hand across Mary's soft face cracked like thunder inside the Schmidt-Johnson family's living room. No one could tell if it was the sound, the pain, or the shock that caused Mary to freeze. After several seconds of stunned paralysis Mary flipped her dinner tray over splattering the food across the floor. She ran outside as quickly as she could, pausing only to grab her school bag before slamming the door shut behind her.

Chapter Three

Mary was perched on the tallest branch that she could climb to on the lone old tree in her backyard. The stars were just beginning to come out, as the sun started to set below the expansive wheat field that bordered her family's backyard. If one didn't know what happened at Mary's dinner earlier that evening, they would have assumed that this was a serene scene.

"Get down from there, Mary!" Friedrich drunkenly yelled, "I just wanna talk!"

Mary hunched over and hugged her school bag tightly. She closed her eyes and imagined that she was somewhere else. *Maybe this is all a terrible dream...* Friedrich stumbled around underneath of the tree. He fidgeted with his now empty beer bottle.

"You're useless, ya know. A goddamn fat-head, like your brother."

Mary hugged her bag even tighter.

"You think you're all high and mighty because you go to school? Think you're too good to help your own mother around the house?"

There was silence for a moment. Did Friedrich give up? Mary listened carefully for a moment. She could no longer hear crunches of dried grass from Friedrich's pacing. She carefully peaked around the trunk of the tree to see if her stepfather was still there.

"You little shit. I knew you were still there. Get your ass down here now!" Friedrich paused for a moment. "Your Mom told me to bring you in to clean up your dinner mess, and that's what I'm going to do!" And with that, he threw the empty beer bottle at Mary.

Mary ducked as the bottle hit the tree. It shattered; the shower of green glass just barely missed her face. Mary took her portable radio out of her school bag and traced her fingers around the inscription that her real father wrote. She turned it up as loudly as it would go and wrapped around it like a safety blanket. Few things in life were as certain as Mary knowing that she would be up there for some time. She figured that she might as well listen to a radio show instead of Friedrich's drunken obscenities.

Mary woke up sometime later, still clutching the radio. The sun had fully set behind the field, and the world was pitch black. She peered around the thick old tree trunk and breathed a sigh of relief to see that Friedrich had gone back into the house. Mary turned the radio off, as the current channel was only receiving static. Everything was silent except for the sound of crickets. *I'm probably the only one still awake in the entire town,* Mary thought to herself.

Just as she prepared to lower herself off the tree branch, a bright blue glow streaked across the sky. *Was it a meteor? An asteroid?* Mary wasn't far enough in school to know the difference yet. Refreshed from her nap and not ready to go home, she decided to chase the glow down and find out for sure what it was. Gripping the rough branch, she lowered herself back to ground. Mary brushed herself off and looked around once more to make sure she wasn't being watched. Now that the coast was clear, it was time for Mary to go on an adventure!

Chapter Four

Saturday, June 14th

The moon was so big and bright that night that it illuminated Mary's path as she sprinted across the neighbouring field. The number of gopher holes that Mary had to dodge reminded her of track class. *Run, run, jump, run, dodge...* Mary wasn't sure what she saw crash in the distance, but she knew she wanted to be the first one there.

Winded and sweaty, Mary finally reached the forest at the end of the field. As bright as the moon was that night, it wasn't strong enough to permeate the thick brush. Mary was always prepared, though. She dug through her school bag and pulled out her clunky old flashlight, another old gift from her father. Mary gave it a shake and listened to the rattle of the bulky D batteries. She wasn't certain that the flashlight would have enough of a charge to last her through the night, but was determined to trudge ahead regardless. Mary looked back over her shoulder at the field before taking a deep breath and stepping into the darkness.

The forest was creepy, even for someone as brave as Mary. *Was that howl from a coyote? Or a wolf? Wendigo? Sasquatch?* Mary needed something to take her mind off her surroundings. She took out her portable radio. Most stations went quiet at night, but Mary knew that without fail she could always listen to a late-night talk show. The shows were not aimed at children, but Mary knew well enough which words she could and couldn't use at home. At least if she played it loudly enough, the banter would keep the wild animals away.

After an arduous trek through the woods, Mary had at last reached the other side. The forest bordered the local quarry. Thankfully the moon was shining brightly enough that the edge was visible. Mary gingerly pushed a small rock over the embankment. *That could have been quite the fall...* The moon shone brightly over the quarry revealing the result of the mysterious glow the Mary was chasing. A real-life spaceship!

The ship was much flimsier looking than the ones she had imagined; it looked like it was made from aluminum foil. *No wonder it crashed,* Mary thought to herself. She couldn't believe her eyes, which began to itch from all the dust in the air. Smoke plumes radiated out of the center of the wrecked flying saucer.

Suddenly, Mary began to hear voices coming from somewhere other than the airwaves. She turned off the radio and crouched behind a boulder. Peering over the top of the rock,

Mary spotted two teenage boys playing amongst the pieces of the crashed ship. She turned away and hid.

"Can ya believe this thing?" Gary hollered as he carelessly tossed around a large strange looking gun.

"Come on, stop it," his friend Phillip begged, as he tried to keep a careful distance.

"Aw come on. I'm just having a gas!" A squirrel ran by, catching the irresponsible boy's eye. "Ooh, free dinner…" The boy raised up the plastic looking gun and aimed at the squirrel the best he could.

"Come on, Gary. It's just a little—"

Expecting a bullet to fire and not a massive energy beam, the force of the weapon's blast knocked Gary off balance. He spun around, ray gun still firing. And with that, Gary's childhood best friend turned into a pile of pink goo. The gelatinous figure, formally known as Phillip, collapsed and splattered everywhere. The backsplash just barely missed the terrified squirrel.

"PHILLIP!" Gary screamed. After a moment of pure terror, he dropped the ray gun and ran away as quickly as he could.

Having missed the commotion while hiding behind the boulder, Mary decided she might as well go in for a closer look now that things had quieted down. She lowered her feet over the side of the quarry and slid down. *Hey, that was kind of fun.* Mary coughed as the dust from the side of the quarry filled her lungs.

The nearly liquified squirrel watched Mary as she walked through the piles of wreckage and towards the slimy pile of

Phillip. Mary stared at the goop curiously, and then the ray gun. *Pile of goop. Ray gun. Pile of goop. Ray gun...* She looked from one to the other before cautiously poking at the pink pile of mucilaginous mess. She debated tasting it, but something in her gut told her that was probably a bad idea.

Mary froze. She could hear the faint crunching of car tires driving across the gravel road into the quarry. The squirrel scurried away, and she realized that she should do the same. She looked around, trying to memorize as much detail as she could of the alien debris. Suddenly, the approaching cars turned on their beacon lights, revealing that they were police cars. Mary hastily grabbed the strange gun from the ground and shoved it into her book bag, before hurrying back up the side of the quarry and into the pitch-black forest.

With only late-night talk radio for company, she sat crossed legged alone on the floor of the shadowy forest. The moss tickled the backs of her legs ever so slightly. At least, she hoped it was the moss and not something with legs. By now her eyes had mostly adjusted to the darkness. Sure, the flashlight could have been a big help, but no matter how scary the forest was Mary was more afraid of police finding her. Her family didn't have a very good relationship the authorities, especially with the local British Columbia Provincial Police.

Mary stared at her book bag intently. She took a deep breath, inhaling the sweet smells of lichen and pine, and undid the claps on the canvas sack. Reaching nervously into the bag, Mary gingerly picked up the ray gun. It was surprisingly heavy for its small size. The gun was glowing faintly, but hopefully not enough to draw attention. She slowly lifted it up to her eye, targeting a lone pine cone that was hanging from a distant branch, just like she had seen Friedrich do while hunting. Mary inhaled deeply to steady herself. Unsure of what to expect, she placed her finger on what looked like the trigger and squeezed gently.

The ray gun charged up briefly before shooting a massive energy bolt out into the forest. The alarming strength of the shot knocked Mary backwards and into the base of a birch tree. Ouch. After the initial stunned feeling wore off, she hoped that the stray energy bolt didn't hit anything in the sky, because she most certainly missed the targeted pine cone.

Several hours later as the sun was beginning to rise, Mary made her way back to her house. Not wanting to wake her mother, or worse, Friedrich, Mary slowly opened the screen door and twisted the handle of the front door as carefully as she could. Friedrich was fast asleep on the couch. He looked peaceful, except for muttering random words in German as he slept. Mary only recognized the word "scheiße." Drinking all day and yelling at children apparently took a lot out of him.

Mary walked cautiously down the hallway, stepping deliberately on just the right spots so as not to make the floorboards creak. On the way to her bedroom, Mary noticed that her mother's bedroom door was open. She paused for a moment and took in the rare view of her mom in a state of rest. She looked so serene.

Finally reaching her own room, Mary placed her school bag next to the bed, slowly laid down, and closed her eyes.

"Mary?" George groggily asked.

"Hey Georgie."

"Where'd you go?"

"I just had to leave for a while," Mary spoke while just on the cusp of sleep.

George paused for a moment, also mid sleep. "I don't like it when you're gone."

"I'm sorry Georgie," Mary spoke carefully.

She could feel a knot forming in her throat and tried desperately not to cry. Mary was a tough kid, but upsetting her brother was a sure-fire way to make her feel weak.

"I get scared."

Mary rolled on her side and faced her brother. *Stay strong, he can't see you upset.* "I don't like leaving you alone here, either."

"Can I come with you, the next time you leave?"

Mary remained silent and waited for George to fall back asleep. She didn't want to lie to him.

Chapter Five

Saturday, June 14th

It was a beautiful morning. Although the sun had just come up, the summer heat was already beginning to radiate through the windows. Having only gone to sleep a couple hours earlier, Mary started to roll over, trying to get the sun out of her eyes, when a small dark figure stood in front of her blocking the sun. She began to drift back to sleep, before she realized that her little brother was staring at her.

"What is it, Georgie?"

"Mom and Bad Daddy are at it again." Not many toddlers had as much practice at sounding exasperated as little George.

"But it's so early…"

"They're talking something about wanting to go hunting… I don't want to go hunting, Mary. Bad Daddy scares me. I, I can garden though!"

Mary bolted out of her bedroom. At least she didn't have to worry about changing out of her pajamas, since she was still in yesterday's clothes. She hurried towards the sound of her parents fighting in the kitchen. As she got closer to the kitchen, she couldn't help but think that her parent's shadows looked like a twisted shadow puppet show.

"I told you, George is too young to go out shootin' all weekend. And Mary's got homework," Margaret barked.

While Mary wasn't happy that her mom was yelling, she was grateful that it sounded like she was defending Mary this time.

"I thought we decided that she wasn't going back to school in the fall? Isn't that what we talked about?" Friedrich yelled, determined to one up Margaret. "You know, I do a whole lotta talking, but no one listens!"

Mary decided to return the favour and defend her mother.

"Leave her alone!" Mary screeched in the way that only a little girl could.

"Jesus girl, don't start with me this early. Grab your things. We're gonna go hunting," Friedrich retorted in a surprisingly nonchalant way. That was the thing about Friedrich, he could go from angry to calm and back again faster than you could say bonkers.

Mary looked to Margaret for assurance.

"Just go with him," she said while averting her gaze, unable to look her daughter in the eyes.

One hour later Mary and Friedrich were sitting in the dried-out field behind their house. Friedrich was perched in a lawn chair, while Mary sat on the ground, using her book bag as a seat. The sun had become even more intense as the morning went on, and Mary wanted nothing more than to go back indoors.

Friedrich leaned over and retrieved a beer from his backpack. The can released a satisfying hiss as Friedrich cracked it open with his teeth. It was marvelous to Mary that such yellowed teeth could still be so strong. Maybe she didn't need to brush her teeth every day after all?

"You've got to learn to provide for this family," Friedrich said to Mary, while staring out into the field.

"I can fish?"

"What, you expect your family to eat fish all day like one of the Japanese? Bah! You should be tried for treason," Friedrich rambled.

Ignoring her drunken stepfather, Mary unzipped her school bag and looked inside. She had brought a few books, in case Friedrich decided to take a nap and she had time, as well as her trusty radio, which had the ray gun tucked behind.

"No one wants to hire women, nor should they. But that doesn't mean you can't learn basic skills to feed your family," Friedrich trailed off as he picked up a long-barreled gun and pointed it towards whatever it was that he had been staring at, all without leaving his chair.

"I could just go to the grocery store, like a normal person?"

"You think they just give you food for free? Besides, people that can't hunt are pansies! A bunch of fruit salads if you ask me. No sense in buying food when there's perfectly good free meat in your own backyard..."

Just then, a gopher popped up from the spot that Friedrich had been fixated on. "There's one! Get it!" Friedrich whisper-yelled, as he passed Mary the gun.

"I really don't want to…"

"Oh, for Christ's sake, kid." Friedrich took the gun back from Mary and fired it at the unsuspecting gopher. The rodent exploded, like a blood-filled water balloon. "Whoopsie daisy! I forgot I was usin' the heavy artillery. You'll wanna use a pellet gun for gophers, or a rifle if you're feeling ambitious."

Friedrich leaned over and picked up another long-barreled gun. Mary hoped it was the correct gun this time; Friedrich owned so many, she understood how it could be confusing. Friedrich creakily got up from his lawn chair and stood over Mary with a gun in each hand, swaying slightly as his breakfast beers began to hit him. "Shot guns are best for things like deer, or people," Friedrich said while gesturing with the gun he used to blow up the gopher. "While pellet guns are for little critters, like vermin or birds," he gestured with what he believed, and Mary hoped, to be a pellet gun.

"Yes-sir-ee, there is a proper gun for each of God's creatures," Friedrich spoke longingly, while lining up another gopher in the pellet gun's sight. Ready, aim, fire. Rather than exploding, this gopher let out a sickening albeit brief squeal. "Well, whatcha waiting for? Go get it."

Mary walked into the dry field, about five yards, to retrieve the dead gopher. It was strange to her that this creature was alive just a minute ago, and now here it was. Dead. She understood that everything must eventually die, and that this was the circle of life, but it was still a morose feeling. Mary stared at it for a moment, before picking up the gopher's lifeless body. It was still warm. Mary wasn't sure if it was because the hot sun or not.

"You. Gotta. Be. Useful!" Friedrich commanded as he slapped Mary on the back of the head; his blows punctuating his words. His already limited patience had clearly worn thin. Mary passed her stepfather the gopher, which he quickly and haphazardly gutted, before placing it in his bloodied old hunting sack. "I swear, everyone in this family is goddamn deaf and dumb. But not in the good way," he mumbled while walking back to his chair.

Once seated Friedrich turned to get another beer, which he proceeded to again crack open with his teeth. Mary thought he would probably pass out soon, so she might as well read. *He killed the gopher, he made whatever point he was trying to make...* She took the book out of her bag and began to read. As soon as she got to the second page, Friedrich spotted the book out of the corner of his eye.

"Put that away. I need your eyes on the field," Friedrich barked as he awkwardly kicked the book out of Mary's hands without leaving his chair. The book landed face down in the dirt just out of Mary's grasp. "School is useless. That's why you're not going back for fourth grade..."

Mary could feel that damn knot forming once again in her throat.

"I told you, you're staying home with your Mom from now on," Friedrich said while finally standing up, as if he was a king making a proclamation. "No women of mine are going to waste their time on useless hobbies like school. I lost my son in the war because he was weak—should'a spent time training instead of reading. I'm not having another weak family!" Friedrich yelled as he kicked over his folding chair throne. He stood over Mary, who was slowly backing up across the dirt.

"Stop cowering!" Friedrich booted Mary in the shins. Tired of being hit, Mary scrambled to her feet and grabbed the ray gun out of her bag. She aimed it at Friedrich.

"Don't touch me."

"Ooh, what's that? A little squirt gun? Got yourself a Water Pistol?" The arrogant false king mocked, while continuing to approach Mary.

"Stay back. I'm serious," Mary demanded.

"Are you threatening me?"

"You keep hurting Mom and George. I'm not going to take it, anymore!"

"Watch your mouth you ungrateful little—"

Before Friedrich could finish cussing out Mary, she fired the ray gun. Friedrich was immediately turned into a large tower of pink goo. As if it was his final attempt to upset her one last time, the Friedrich-shaped tower of goo collapsed onto Mary, splattering everywhere as if someone had dropped a massive aspic salad. The goo coated Mary from head to toe and hit everything within a ten-foot radius: the discarded book, the folding chair, and even an onlooking gopher.

Mary stood in wide-eyed shock for what felt like forever before wiping a huge glob of the disgusting gunk from her face and flicking it onto the ground.

Chapter Six

Mary stood on the front steps of her house. She looked down at her clothes, which were still coated in a disgusting pink goo. While it looked like she was coated in a gelatinous dessert, it most certainly didn't smell that way. The smell was metallic, which makes sense since the goop was made up of Mary's melted stepfather… Mary knew she was going to get in trouble for this. She took a deep breath to prepare herself for her encounter with her mom and gagged from the smell.

"MARY! What in high hell happened to you?" Margaret screamed.

Mary had hoped she could make her to way to the washroom to get cleaned up before telling her mother what happened, but not everything goes according to plan. Her mother sprinted over from the kitchen with a tea towel and immediately began cleaning Mary's face. She sort of enjoyed the attention but couldn't help but think that her mother just didn't want Mary to get the floor dirty.

"What did you and your father get up to?" Margaret asked while crouching down to Mary's level.

"I..." Mary was hesitant to admit that she shot her stepfather with a ray gun; it wasn't exactly an easy topic for anyone, let alone a nine-year-old, to bring up. "I got sick of him hurting us, Mama."

Margaret stopped picking pieces of her husband out of Mary's hair and looked her daughter straight in the eyes, "What do you mean?"

"That man you married. I got tired of him always hittin' me." This time it was Mary who couldn't look her mother in the eyes. She felt guilty, even though she was protecting herself. What was this feeling?

Margaret sprang to her feet. "What did you do, Mary?"

"I uh, I found this thing the other night. I kept it, because it looked neat," Mary took the ray gun out of her bag. "When he tried to touch me again today, I used it."

Margaret began to back away from Mary, trembling. "What did you do to your father?"

"Stop calling him that!" Mary hollered, while still looking at the ground.

"What did you do?!" Margaret shrieked.

"I used this," Mary held up the ray gun, as if it was any old trinket. "It turned him into gelatin," she said as she flicked a glob of Friedrich onto the floor.

Margaret had already backed up as far as she could and now had her back up against the wall. Mary couldn't understand why her mom was acting this way. "Mom, it's okay! Now he can't hurt us anymore! He's just Jell-O!"

George cautiously walked into the room. "Is Bad Daddy gone?"

"George, go to your room!" Margaret screamed at the confused toddler.

George looked to Mary for approval, the confusion in his little face mirroring his sister's internal feelings.

"It's okay. Listen to Mom."

"It is absolutely not okay! My baby is a killer! A lunatic!" Margaret choked out. She had started to cry.

"But he always hurt you!" Mary shouted, confounded.

"So what? That man provided for us! How'd you think we keep a roof over our heads? That man paid for everything!"

Mary looked around at her family's decrepit house. "He wasn't doing a good job of it though—"

Before she could finish her sentence, Margaret leaned in and slapped her.

Crack.

"You think you know what's good for this family, huh? Get out of here then! Leave!"

"But Mama, I was just protecting us—"

"Leave!" Margaret yelled at the top of her lungs.

"You're lucky I don't call the authorities on you!" Margaret added as Mary ran away, the screen door swinging behind her.

Once outside, Mary snuck around to the other side of the house. She hopped up and tapped on her bedroom window to get George's attention. "Georgie! Georgie!" Mary whisper-yelled as loudly as she could between jumps.

George, always the loyal brother, opened the window. "What happened Mary? Did you say Bad Dad is gone now?"

"Yes, he's gone. He's… Not coming back."

"Why is Mom mad then?"

Mary paused for a moment, "Adults are complicated. Hey Georgie, could you throw me my camping stuff?"

George left the window for a moment before running back with a duffel bag roughly twice his size. He awkwardly flipped the bag out of the window. "Why do you need this? Can I come with you?"

"Mom's pretty mad so I've got to go for a bit. I'll come home soon though, okay?"

"You promise?"

"I promise."

George hung out of the window with his pinky finger extended. Mary stood on her tippy toes and reached as far as she could. She managed to grab her brother's hand and accepted his pinky swear.

"Wait!" George hurried away from the window. He returned moments later with his stuffed bear, which he dropped down to Mary. "Take Mister Purdy with you. He will keep you safe."

Chapter Seven

After being kicked out of the house, Mary once again found herself hiding out in the forest. The intimidatingly deep, dark forest was much more welcoming in the day. The branches that only twelve hours ago resembled dismembered arms reaching out from the shadows now only looked like, well, tree limbs. In fact, during daylight hours, the forest was actually quite pleasant. Mary could see where she was walking, and knew that the creatures that went bump in the night were only squirrels and songbirds. Although, if she did happen upon a chupacabra or sasquatch, Mary was confident she'd think of an escape plan.

Mary dropped the extremely heavy camping bag that had begun to cut into her shoulder, and hurried towards the creek which ran through the middle of the forest. Crouching over the small stream, Mary splashed water on herself and did her best to wash away all the remaining slime. The freezing cold water in the creek stung her face; she wasn't aware that she had gotten sunburnt while out hunting with Friedrich. Once she was as cleaned up as she was going to be, she took a few minutes to take in her surroundings. The trees were thick enough to provide cover, but also sparse enough in spots to let in a few rays of sun. There was a nearby saskatoon berry bush, and a few patches of wild strawberries. And the best part, there were no adults or bullies for miles. Other than the temperature of the water, this was going to be a perfect place for Mary to set-up camp. She also really didn't want to carry the camping supplies any further if it could be helped.

Mary reached into the bag and pulled out a spool of rope and a small tarp. She pushed against two spindly nearby trees to test their strength. After shaking and kicking them and doing all she could to mimic a wind storm, Mary was satisfied with the spot that she picked, and used the rope to hang the tarp between the two trees. She was going to be quite comfortable here, unless it snowed. Mary knew that was extremely unlikely to happen in June, but she always liked to be prepared.

Once the tarp was strung up, Mary made a clearing underneath. She brushed away the twigs and pine needles, revealing a smooth dusty patch. She retrieved a small wool blanket from the camping bag, which she laid out underneath the tarp. It was almost perfect, but something was still missing. Mary felt around, checking out the contents of the bag. *What else is in here,* she wondered. A fishing rod, and some hooks. Ouch! A mug. A coffee percolator... Eventually she pulled out George's teddy bear, Mr. Purdy. She placed the scruffy old teddy bear on the blanket and smiled.

Mary sat down next to the bear and stared out at the creek. For what felt like the first time in her short life, she finally had a moment of peace. She took the slightly gooey book out of her book bag and began to read. After only a few pages though, the hairs on the back of Mary's neck stood up as she began to sense that something was watching her...

A breathy moan was coming from behind the saskatoon berry bush.

Arrrrooooooaaaggghhhh...

Mary froze. *Was it a bear? A cougar? A pervert?* Mary's Mom had warned her about all three, but she was never told what to do if she was confronted by one.

Never one to run away from danger, Mary retrieved a small pocket knife from a pouch in the camping bag. It took Mary a moment to remember that she had something so much better than a small knife. She tossed the scuffed up old Swiss Army knife aside and grabbed the ray gun.

Holding the ray gun in front of her, like she saw a cop do in a movie once, Mary carefully crept towards the groaning shrubbery, and used her foot to kick away part of the bush revealing what was making the sound. Expecting a wild animal, Mary couldn't believe her eyes when she came face to face with what appeared to be... an alien. It was lanky and grey, with hints of blue scales. Or was that its suit? Anyone else would have been terrified, but Mary recognized the pain in the alien's giant brown eyes. They reminded her of a cow's eyes, gentle.

"Hello," Mary spoke softly.

The alien continued to breathe deeply, in pain. Mary could tell that it wasn't a threat.

"I'm Mary… What is your name?"

The wounded alien looked up at her. Its breathing slowed.

"I'm not going to hurt you." As Mary spoke those words, she sensed that didn't need to say them out loud; the alien understood her somehow.

Mary looked around and found a thick branch which must have blown down in the last big windstorm. Spotting the pocket knife she cast aside moments before, she picked it up and opened the blade, causing the alien to wince slightly.

"It's okay," Mary said softly, never taking her eyes off the alien, making sure it was watching as she started to scrape some off some of the rough bark. She put the knife away, and offered the branch to the alien. "Here, it's to help you walk."

Mary reached towards the alien and tried to help it stand up. It was only then that she realized the extent of its injuries. Its leg was bleeding, but its most severe injury was its missing hand. Mary couldn't help but notice that the alien had red blood. The men performing the radio shows always talked about little green men from Mars. She never would have expected an alien to have the same fluids as a human.

Realizing that the first aid kit in her camping bag was out of band aids and gauze, thanks to a mysterious hunting incident with Friedrich weeks prior that she knew little about, Mary ripped the sleeves off her plaid printed button up shirt. The sleeves were still wet from earlier, but they would be better than nothing. She had worn a long-sleeved shirt out hunting so that she wouldn't get sun burnt while out with Friedrich, completely forgetting that her face was exposed. She imaged that by now, she probably looked like a tomato.

Mary slowly reached towards the alien's wounded arm. "Could I see your arm please? We need to stop the bleeding."

Mary gently, but tightly, made a tourniquet out of her shirt sleeves. She wrapped the first one around the alien's wrist and the second one around its injured shin. The alien let out a series of odd clicking noises and gestured towards the quarry. Through their innate shared understanding of one another, Mary helped the alien to stand up and led it to the gravel quarry where she had found the space ship wreckage the night before.

After slowly making their way through the forest, Mary and the alien found themselves at the edge of the quarry embankment. All the wreckage was gone, as if nothing had ever happened. Mary and the alien looked to one another, knowingly. "It's okay, you can stay with me."

Hand in hand, Mary and the alien walked back into the forest.

Chapter Eight

Mary kneeled next to the alien, who was sitting by the stream at Mary's encampment. Its long thin legs stretched out in front of it, the alien was at least seven feet tall with a surprisingly short torso. Mary had the contents of her first aid kit spread out along the rocks. It contained a small pair of scissors, a scalpel, material to craft a splint, cotton balls, iodine, and even several ration packets. She used to think it was weird that her late stepfather would shop at military surplus stores, but now she was happy that he had. Other than its lack of bandaging, the kit had nearly everything one might need if they came across someone injured in the woods. Even if that person was from outer space.

"Let me see your arm," Mary said while gesturing to the alien's wounded stump. The alien cautiously extended its arm as Mary slowly poured a cup of water over the alien's injury.

"We need to clean it out."

The alien let out a series of clicks, indicating that it was in pain.

"I'm so sorry. It's going to get worse," Mary said as she retrieved a bottle of iodine from the kit, before gently dabbing it on the alien's wound with a cotton ball.

CLICK CLICK CLICK CLICK...

Chapter Nine

Sunday, June 15th

The sun was beaming through the windows of the Schmidt family's single floor rancher. The light refracted off the little bits of dust that were lazily floating in the air. Some of Margaret's busybody friends had made comments about the state of the house, but they just didn't understand that dust was natural, and that's just what happened when you had kids running in and out of the house all day and you lived next to a farmyard. At least that's what Margaret told herself.

It was the early afternoon, and Margaret was resting with her feet up. With her abusive husband recently vaporized, and her uppity daughter ousted to the forest, this was the first time in years that she was able to lay back and relax with a magazine. *Sure, I'm probably going to have nightmares about this ordeal for the rest of my life, but what family doesn't have issues,* Margaret rationalized. The ever-present George was usually annoying, but had seemed to have gotten the hint that he should be quiet and focus on his colouring books that day. Margaret needed some me time.

Margaret closed the previous month's edition of Chatelaine on her chest and without looking, picked up the glass of lemonade that she had sitting on the floor. She had considered spicing up the drink and adding some liquor to it, but she personally wasn't much of a drinker. After being married to that drunk Friedrich, for three – nearly four years – the smell of alcohol made her sick. Her first husband Douglas wasn't much of a drinker either, which is why his liver cancer diagnosis had been so shocking.

Margaret took a long sip of the tart lemonade and placed the drink on the floor, then reopened the magazine and continued to read. She didn't much care for Chatelaine as she thought it was too feminine, but there weren't many other options for sale at the local general store. No sooner than Margaret started the next article, than there was a knock at the door.

"Can you go get that for Mama, Georgie?"

Annoying or not, sometimes it was helpful to have a small butler. Not to be a pessimist, but Margaret knew she would never be wealthy. Especially since she left most of her belongings back in Ukraine when she migrated here. Not wanting her own kids to go through the struggles of learning a second language, she never spoke her mother tongue at home. She rationalised that most children weren't smart enough to learn more than one language anyway. It had been so difficult to start a new life alone when she was just fifteen, that now that she was grown, it was fun for her to pretend that she had a little servant.

Little Georgie hopped up from the carpeted floor, accidentally spilling his box of pencil crayons in the process. "Yes, Mama."

Margaret was proud of how obedient her son was; she didn't know that he only listened because he was afraid of being kicked out of the house like his older sister. George hastily ran to the front of the house and opened the screen door for the two stately looking men that were on the other side.

"Why, hello there little guy! Is your daddy home?" Constable Stone, a stocky middle-aged man, asked.

"My dad is dead. He died a long time ago," George responded sadly, holding back tears. He didn't understand why a stranger would show up only to ask him something so mean. Not only that, but the constable's large mustache made him uncomfortable. It reminded him of something that their old cat used to leave on the front step.

"Oh. I'm sorry little fella…" Constable Stone turned to his partner, "Maybe this is the wrong house?"

The second agent, District Game Warden Smith, a clean cut and much more strong jawed man than his partner, crouched down in front of George.

"We're asking about this man," Warden Smith asked, flashing George a photo of Friedrich.

"Oh! You mean Bad Daddy. He isn't home right now," George said as he choked back tears.

Margaret abruptly stepped in front of George. To the officers, it might have appeared that she was protecting her son, but she really just wanted her toddler son to stop blathering. Their family was already the talk of the town; Margaret didn't want everyone to know that her daughter was also a killer. "Why hello officers. What seems to be the problem?"

"Hello, ma'am. We are looking for your husband. Friedrich Johnson," Warden Smith said while standing up. His knees cracked, and he resented having to bend down to talk to a child in the first place.

"Can I ask why?" Margaret asked hesitantly.

"We have reports that he has been participating in some extremely *illicit* activity," Constable Stone spoke under a hushed breath. The word illicit caused the constable's moustache to flare out ever so slightly.

"What has he done this time?" Margaret could feel the hair on the back of her neck begin to prickle.

"He was reported for killing innocent—"

"Poaching, ma'am. Your husband is a poacher," Warden Smith bluntly announced before his partner could continue.

"Poaching? Whew. I thought you were gonna say that he hurt someone," Margaret rubbed her arms in nervous relief.

"Poaching *is* serious. That's why the Game Department was established," Warden Smith scolded.

"Yeah, if your husband had robbed a bank or caused bodily harm to a person, then the BCPP would be here right now—" Constable Stone rambled on.

"Where is your husband?" his boss, Warden Smith, interrupted.

Warden Smith knew that he cast a much more imposing figure than his subordinate and was not afraid to embrace it.

"Maybe this is all a misunderstanding that he can clear up?" Constable Stone offered sympathetically to Margaret, while giving his superior officer a sideways glance.

Wow, they must've practiced this "Mutt and Jeff" routine, Margaret thought to herself. She looked down at the rusty old stain on the floor right by the door, left behind from Friedrich's constantly leaking hunting bag.

"Oh, no. It's not a misunderstanding. He definitely did it," Margaret finally spoke.

"Sh-shooting on protected lands?" Constable Stone sputtered, taken back by Margaret's nonchalant attitude.

"Oh yeah."

"Raiding the neighbours hen house?" Warden Smith asked with a raised eyebrow.

"Sounds like Friedrich."

"Did he also shoot that poor gorilla at the zoo?" Constable Stone asked, his moustache continuing to sway with each word.

"That one, probably not."

"Your husband sounds like a real piece of work, ma'am. Where is he?" Warden Smith asked, while opening a small black notebook.

"I'd turn him in in a heartbeat, but I haven't seen him in two days."

"Why not?" Warned Smith asked with a raised eyebrow. He couldn't imagine a husband not coming home to his wife every night. Unless the husband was a good for nothing debaucher.

That is a good question. Margaret paused for a moment, thinking up a believable backstory. What would be believable, but also not cause the townspeople to think any worse of her… "I heard a rumour he took off with that gal down at the corner store. He was always philandering. For all his faults, Friedrich was—is—still quite a charmer."

Warden Smith looked at the picture of Friedrich that he had shown George moments ago, with a raised eyebrow. Based off his appearance, Warden Smith wouldn't have described Friedrich as a charmer. *Maybe Constable Stone was right, maybe I do judge people too quickly.* Realizing he was getting distracted, Smith fixed his posture and cleared his throat, "Mind if we take a look inside?"

"I'd tell you if he was here," Margaret said, as kindly as she could without being defensive. She perfected this tone in her last relationship.

"We just need to be certain." Warden Smith stepped past Margaret, and into the house. Constable Stone followed his boss, while mouthing the words *I am so sorry* to Margaret.

Warden Smith and Constable Stone were both taken back by the situation in the Schmidt house. Large stacks of newspapers were piled up on a dinner tray. The lone house plant had clearly been used as an ashtray. Several stray beer tins were sitting in the corner of the room. And in the center of it all, little George was sprawled out across the thick green carpeting, colouring. The officers looked to each other knowingly, as if they were making a secret pact to each other to never complain about how clean their wives kept their own houses ever again.

"What does your husband do for a living, Miss—"

"It's Margaret," Margaret interrupted Constable Stone. "Anyway, he doesn't do much. Hunting mostly. Or poaching, as you gentlemen are now calling it."

Warden Smith crouched down next to George stiffly. "Who's that in the picture, son?"

"You're not great with kids, are you, boss?" Constable Stone asked, turning away from Margaret to address his boss.

"This is me. This is my mom. This is my sister, Mary. And this is Bad Daddy as a pile of goo!" George explained, excitedly.

"Kids are so creative—" Margaret justified.

"And where is your sister at right now?" Warden Smith said, interrupting Margaret. "Can we talk to her?"

"Oh, no. Mary's gone now. Mommy made her leave." George's enthusiasm faded as he remembered that Mary was no longer at home. He looked back at his paper, and returned to drawing.

"Your mother kicked out your sister?" Constable Stone asked with concern,

Sensing that things were going south, Margaret once again stepped between George and the officers. "It feels like you're asking a lot of questions! Why don't you come back later? I'll bake a pie. Lemon curd? Do you like lemon—"

Ignoring Margaret, Warden Smith continued to try to speak with George. "Why don't you tell me about your sister?"

"Her name is Mary. She's my big sister, and I love her very much. Mommy doesn't though, so she made Mary live in the forest."

"Like you said, kids are so creative?" Constable Stone offered to Margaret.

"No, he's right. Mary is such a little survivalist, trying to be like Jacque Cousteau, or James Cook…? One of those people that school shoved down her throat. So, she went out camping. She'll be home later."

The officers looked at each other, and then to Margaret.

"Well, that sounds fine to me. After all, we're here on poaching charges. Not anything about your children," Warden Smith said with a shrug.

"As long as you make sure she is home tonight, it should be fine, I guess… Please telephone us when Friedrich comes home though," Constable Stone asked, while following Warden Smith out of the house.

Margaret followed the officers and locked the door behind them. She returned to the living room, where she shot George an angry glare.

"Did I do something wrong?"

"Go back to colouring."

Margaret laid back down on the couch. She had lost her place in the magazine. Frustrated, she leaned over and picked up her glass of lemonade which had gotten warm.

"Can I go visit Mary?" George said while putting his art supplies away.

Margaret could feel the vein in the side of her head start to throb. She closed her eyes and did her best to imagine that she was on a beach somewhere tropical and far away.

Chapter Ten

Most kids that had been kicked out of their homes would panic and plead for their parents' forgiveness. Not Mary though. While her mother dealt with the conservation officers and chores back home, Mary was in her element. She had her fishing gear, a new friend, and her radio. What more did a kid need?

From dawn until dusk, Mary worked to teach the alien outdoor skills. She didn't know how long that they would be out here together for and thought that she might as well teach the alien everything that she knew about surviving in the woods. What if the alien had forests back home and got lost again one day? Mary wanted it to be prepared. Although she would never admit it out loud, Mary had learned a few useful things from Friedrich over the years, and now that he was dead it felt like she should share some of that knowledge.

The two of them went fishing, fastened spears, and exchanged stories of each of their life's adventures. Mary still wasn't quite sure how she understood the alien; she had heard about this sort of communication before, in a radio show about gypsies and psychics, but word escaped her. Cards on the table though, if Mary had to pick one favourite moment from the day, it was when the two of them were sitting together at the camp enjoying the music from the radio.

Night was going to be there soon, and it was starting to get cold. Even though Falkland was in the middle of a semi-arid desert and got quite hot during the summer months, it could become chilly at night. Unbeknownst to her, the ray gun had a mode which made it shoot an electrical beam rather than turning its target gelatinous. The alien showed her this feature and used it to start a small fire when it became obvious that the one-handed alien was never going to be able to start a fire by rubbing two twigs together.

By dark, the two friends had worked up quite an appetite. They had tried hunting for rabbit, but it didn't go well as this was before the alien taught Mary about the ray gun's electrical mode. Thankfully they managed to catch several trout, as the accidental batch of rabbit Jell-O was nauseating. Mary sliced the fish open and skewered them on two green branches. The branches needed to be fresh, otherwise they would catch fire and ruin dinner. Mary had also soaked them in the water before hand, just to be safe. Once the fish scales began to turn crispy and peel off of the fish, Mary took them off of the fire.

"I'm sorry. I didn't pack any dishes," Mary spoke softly as she passed a trout to the alien.

Although she had never seen the alien open its mouth, Mary assumed that it at least had one. It took her by surprise though to see the alien's small facial slit stretch open widely enough to fit the entire fish in its mouth and swallow it whole. Mary was thankful it was dark out, because seeing the alien's surprisingly toothy mouth in all the detail of daylight might have finally scared her.

Sensing Mary's discomfort, the alien opened its mouth again, reached down its throat, and pulled out the still-intact fish skeleton and carefully offered it back to Mary. It clearly didn't want to come across as rude.

After dinner, Mary bathed in the frigid creek. The one thing she didn't have in her bag was a tooth brush, so Mary had used her finger and some berries for flavour. It didn't work as well as she had hoped, and now she had seeds stuck in her teeth. After splashing around in the chilly water, Mary cozied up with the alien next to the fire. There was a clearing in the trees just above the camp which allowed the sky to show through. The night sky was strewn with stars, as if a handful of glitter had gotten stuck in the sky. Mary looked at the alien in wonder. "Which star did you come from?"

The alien looked up to the sky. It sat in thought for a moment, before pointing to a star in the Orion Constellation.

"Your home is in that cluster?"

The alien drew a circle in the air and moved its hand through it.

"A planet that moves through it?" Mary paused for a moment, thinking carefully about her next question.

"I don't want to seem dumb, but I've got to know. What is the difference between a star and a planet? We haven't gotten that far in school yet."

The alien let out a series of quiet clicking sounds. Mary nodded, knowingly. The two continued to stare off into the stars letting the world around them disappear.

"When your friends come back, I hope I can go with you."

The alien carefully wrapped its good arm around Mary. She tried to rest her head on its shoulder but was only able to reach its elbow. Either way, this was the most comfortable she had ever felt. Although Mary knew that no one would believe her if she told them about the alien's home world, she took pride in being the only person on Earth to know something so special.

Chapter Eleven

Friday, June 20th

Susan Webb stood in front of her less-than-interested third grade class. She understood that children that age didn't always have the longest attention spans, but she still wished that they would at least pretend to listen to her more. Even though the class only had ten students in it, they could get quite rambunctious. Being disrespected was probably one of Susan's biggest pet peeves, but she resigned herself to the fact that was just life. Besides, these children couldn't help it; some of them had terrible parents. Or rather, most did. But Susan would never share that thought out loud.

Her late-ex-fiancé Douglas and she had been planning on having children, but their life together didn't turn out as planned. They were high school sweethearts who had moved to Falkland in 1937, shortly before the second World War began. As an Engineering Officer with the United States Army, Douglas was privy to news about global events before the general public. Sensing that international troubles were brewing, and knowing that army desertion was a capital offence, Douglas had convinced Susan to start over in Falkland with him. All they had to do was change their last names. However, once they arrived in Falkland, Douglas was quickly entranced by one of the local harlots. Susan knew the only reason he would ever betray her is if he just couldn't help it. Deep down she knew that he loved her...

Because of that unmet maternal longing, Susan was passionate about imparting as much knowledge as she could onto her students. At least today's science class subject was outer space. That, and dinosaurs, always got the most interest. It also gave her an excuse to wear her fantastic planet patterned dress that she sewed for herself last summer. Back in Tacoma, Susan had planned on becoming a seamstress.

"So, thanks to Sir Isaac Newton's discovery in 1687, we understand that our moon actually controls the tides of the ocean. How interesting is that?" Susan exclaimed perhaps a little too excitedly. She cleared her throat, realizing that her voice was coming across as more perturbed than necessary. "Does anyone have any questions so far?"

"What is the difference between stars and planets?" Mary asked, only raising her arm half way in an attempt to shield her increasingly tattered shirt.

While she preferred when students waited until they were called on directly to ask a question, Susan was happy to see that Mary Schmidt was participating. Although Mary was one of Susan Webb's best students, there were days when she seemed distracted or afraid to speak up. It gave Susan hope each time that Mary would assert herself. That child would always have a soft spot in Susan's heart. If Douglas hadn't been so overcome with lust for that awful Margaret woman, Mary might have wound up in Susan's womb. She was worried at how scruffy Mary looked today though; it was as if she had been rolling around in dirt all week. "That's a great question, Mary. Stars produce their own light because of radiation, and planets orbit around them. Planets also don't produce their own light."

Mary smiled, happy to know that the alien was right and that she hadn't misunderstood it. Unable to allow her to have this lone moment of reprieve, the class bullies decided that now was the time to start mocking Mary. It was as though they shared their own psychic connection.

"Planets orbit stars the way gross men orbit Mary's Mom!" Don yelled out. Not content with merely tripping Mary down the school steps, he had to take her down in class too.

"Don, go to the principal's office," Susan sighed.

The rest of the class chuckled, causing Don to blush. The chubby bully stood up. His increasingly pink babylike face betraying the tough guy image he tried to present. "Worth it," Don muttered, as he left the class.

Susan looked at the class with as stern a glare as she could muster. She wished she looked more authoritative, but resigned herself to the fact that she just wasn't that kind of person. "Moving on... The ninth planet in our solar system is Pluto. This little planet was discovered very recently actually.

In 1930! Some of your parents were probably sitting in these very same desks when the discovery was made."

"Mary's parents didn't even go to school," Lucy, the curly blonde-haired preacher's daughter and passionate tormentor of Mary, snarked.

"Do you want to go to the office too, Lucy?"

"What is past Pluto?" a shy student from the back of the class asked.

"Nothing that we know of, yet. Pluto was only discovered seventeen years ago though, so just think what else could be out there!" Susan exclaimed with a restrained excitement; she really did love to teach about space.

Mary raised her hand. Her earlier confidence staring to fade.

"Yes Mary?"

"I, um, heard that there is a tenth planet."

"Where did you hear that?"

"Just, from a friend."

"Mary, we all know you don't have friends," Lucy called out.

"Lucy, go sit in the hall."

Lucy shot Mary a smirk as she walked out of the classroom. Because of the rule of threes, the third bully, Ricky, the one that looked like his hair was slicked with motor oil, used this time to make a kissy face at Mary. She knew that it meant she was a butt kisser – there was no way that either of those two gross boys would ever flirt with her.

Noticing that it was almost three o'clock, Susan decided that she should end this class. Besides, as much as she loved space, the brats in this class were starting to get exhausting.

"That's all for today though, class," Susan called out, "Don't forget that your dioramas are due next week. This is your last project of the year, so it's extra important!"

With her head down, Mary nearly snuck out of the classroom unnoticed. Susan managed to catch her just in time.

"Mary, could I talk with you?"

"What is the problem, Miss Webb?" There was a weariness to Mary's eyes that made her teacher even more concerned than normal.

To Susan it looked as if Mary had been sleeping rough. "There's no problem. I am just wondering how you are. How things are with you and your Mom?"

"Oh, you know..." Mary looked down at her feet, hesitant to reveal too much. She noticed how dirty her shoes were, and started kicking little bits of clay off, onto the wooden classroom floor.

"You're not in trouble. I promise. I am just worried because you are turning into a little," Susan searched for the right word, "A little bit of a ragamuffin, and I want to make sure that things are okay at home. I understand that sometimes your parents, um, get distracted from their parenting duties."

"It's fine," Mary insisted. "I've been staying with a friend."

"Is that the friend that told you about the planet past Pluto?"

Mary didn't respond. She continued to kick off flecks of dirt from her sneakers.

"How do you know this person, Mary?"

"I need to go, Miss Webb. Thank you for looking out for me. I'm fine though. Promise." Mary turned and hurried away, leaving Susan Webb even more concerned than she already was.

Chapter Twelve

Saturday, June 21st

It was a Saturday morning just like every other Saturday morning for the Bishop family. The three of them were gathered around their over sized oak dining room table for their weekly family breakfast. In front of each family member was a similarly laid out plate of slightly burnt bacon, sunny side up eggs, and apple butter toast. The entire house had a slight maple scent from the syrup that the family matriarch, Helen, would add to the bacon. Some people might have called this breakfast excessive. For the Bishops however, this was routine. All little Lucy Bishop really wanted to eat though was a damned bowl of cereal.

Be present at our table, Lord.

Be here and everywhere adored.

Thy people bless, and grant that we,

may feast in paradise with thee.

Lucy's father, Raymond Bishop, the town's preacher, always insisted on saying this prayer before breakfast. Sometimes they would forget to do it before their nightly dinners, but Helen and Raymond insisted that Saturday morning family breakfast was treated with the utmost importance. Since Raymond worked Sundays and left the house early during the week, it was the one day that they had free to spend together as a family. Lucy often ate dinners alone, or in the kitchen with her mother. She didn't understand the importance of seeing her father on Saturdays and was apathetic about the entire ritual.

Raymond wasn't always a man of God. In fact, he used to be a real estate agent in the nearby town of Vernon. He wasn't the most reputable realtor in the region though, and he had burned a lot of bridges. Not necessarily because Raymond was a bad person; he was only trying to get ahead the best that he knew how. When the Great Depression hit, Raymond and his wife, Helen, took this as an opportunity to get out of Dodge and moved to Falkland. The town was just starting to grow and felt like the perfect place for a fresh start. No one knew them yet, and there were very few people for them to get to know. Life would be easy.

Raymond had decided to become a preacher once he learned that Protestant preachers did not need to be ordained, unlike their pastoral counterparts. Most of the townspeople didn't realize that though, and because he was such a charismatic man, he quickly settled into his new role. Lucy was born nearly five years after the Bishop's moved to Falkland, although it wasn't for their lack of trying... Her parents were so proud of their precocious little girl. She was their greatest prize. Their little golden child. Her blonde curls were identical to her mothers, while she shared her father's blue eyes.

When Lucy grew older, she would grow to think that Helen and Raymond felt comfortable talking with her as an adult because of everything they projected on her. To them though, they simply wanted her to know how much she was loved, even though Lucy found their prayers and old person stories to be incredibly dull.

Lucy picked at her breakfast, as she did every Saturday: a few bites of bacon here, a few bites of toast there. Her mother would throw the rest of it in the garbage shortly after Lucy slid her plate to the center of the table and left the house to go and find either Don or Ricky. Neither of them ever had weekend family events to attend. Lucy liked that about them.

Chapter Thirteen

While the Bishop family had their Saturday breakfast, and Mary was up to who knows what, Margaret was sunbathing in the front lawn. Growing sick of the dust in the house, Margaret had been spending more and more time outside in the sun. It was so refreshing to not have a family to take care of. Yes, George was still around, but he mostly kept to himself. At this moment, he was teaching himself how to do flips on the rusty old tire swing. As long as he stayed quiet, Margaret was content. Except for the persistent hum of insects in the tall dry grass, life was silent. Stretched out so far that she only her upper torso remained in the lawn chair, Margaret let out the occasional sigh. *This is the life.*

Just as Margaret was about to doze off, she was startled by a loud ding ding ding! She shot up out of her seat, and spotted Susan Webb, Mary's teacher and Margaret's nemesis biking towards her. *Ugh, of course she would put a bell on her bicycle,* Margaret thought to herself. Susan was so clingy. So hopelessly needy. In Ukraine, they called women like Susan коза –

roughly translated to "annoying goat" – but Margaret would never speak her first language here. It was safer this way.

Margaret's first husband, the father of her children and the real love of her life, Douglas had moved to Falkland to escape from Susan. She knew that Susan and Douglas were high school sweethearts, but as he told her, their relationship had soured as the years went on. He told Susan that he had to move to Canada, to escape the war. An impending war was a silly excuse he made up to escape her; Douglas didn't think that one would actually take place. He told Margaret how guilty he felt, as if he had willed this into being, while reading about the rise of Hitler in the newspaper. At the time Douglas was just a silly boy who wanted to be free from his girlfriend – he never thought Susan would follow him all of the way to Falkland, but when he arrived in town, she was already here! Not only had she pursued him all of the way from the United States into Canada, but she had somehow managed to arrive there before him. The woman was relentless.

"Marg! Hi! I hope I'm not disturbing you..." Susan trailed off as she dismounted from her bicycle. The bike was blue and matched perfectly with her gingham print sun dress. Susan was always dressed for the occasion, no matter what that occasion may be. Margaret liked to joke that Susan would dress up for the opening of an envelope.

"Susan Webb... I haven't seen you in ages." Margaret scoffed, while standing up.

"You'd see more of me if you came to Mary's parent teacher meetings," Susan replied in a saccharinely sweet tone that Margaret detested.

"What do you want? What did Mary do this time?" Margaret eyed Susan up and down. She figured that she could beat her in a fistfight, if she had to.

"Mary hasn't done anything. Is she here though? I'd love to say hi," Susan said as she peered around the yard.

"No. She's out camping." Margaret really disliked how close Susan tried to be with Mary. It made her deeply uncomfortable.

Susan continued to look around at the Schmidt property. She knew Margaret had a difficult life, having only migrated to Canada in the 1930s, but thought that Margaret should work harder to keep a tidy house. After all, as Susan always said, a clean home is the mark of a clean mind. She would never understand what attracted so many men, including Susan's former fiancé, to this woman. "Camping just for the weekend, or something more permanent?"

"Who knows. Children these days do what they want." Margaret didn't like what Susan was insinuating, even if it was true. She knew that she wasn't the perfect parent but didn't need it to be rubbed in her face every waking moment of the day.

"Okay, I'll cut to the chase. I'm here because Mary looks like she hasn't been bathing lately, and I just wanted to make sure that she is being taken care of."

Margaret shrugged, "Kids get dirty outside."

George walked up behind Margaret and gave her leg a big hug.

Susan crouched down to George's eye level, which was also level to Margaret's knee. "Hi Georgie. Do you remember when you last saw your sister?"

"Seven days ago. I know, because I count. Mom, can I have a snack?" George asked, changing his focus from Susan Webb to his mother.

"Why are you asking me? You know where to find them," Margaret shook George off her leg and shooed him away. She momentarily debated kneeing Susan in the face but thought better of it.

"A week feels like a long time for a little girl to be out camping with friends."

"Friends? Pfff, my Mary doesn't have friends. She's out there alone. She's tough, like her mom."

"No one has ever suggested otherwise, Margaret."

"I know not everyone likes me. Some women get envious that I can land a man so easily," Margaret replied defensively.

"You slept with my fiancé," Susan spoke bluntly. There it was, that horrible thing that Susan always tried to forget about and yet somehow thought about every single day.

"Oh, that's right, Douglas was with you first. I always forget. He was such an honorable man though, to marry me when I fell pregnant with Mary."

"You didn't deserve Douglas, and you certainly don't deserve a daughter as bright as Mary," Susan rebutted.

Although the two women were speaking outside, the atmosphere felt as tense as an elastic band that was ready to snap. By now, both Margaret and Susan were standing toe to toe. The contrast between them was striking. Susan was smiley, blonde, and slight, while Margaret had dark, nearly black hair, broad shoulders, and a permanently tired look on her face. While nearly the exact same age, to onlookers it would have been quite clear to which one of them had seemingly lived multiple lives.

Margaret broke the tension with a laugh. She honestly couldn't remember the last time she made that sound. Her sharp-yet-sarcastic chuckle caused the metaphorical elastic band of tension to snap and hit Susan in the face. Susan backed up, appalled. "Sounds like envy to me, Susan. Is that all? Is there anything else you want to talk about?" Margaret barked, unwavering in her stance.

"Mary needs to show up to class clean on Monday, or else I am reporting you to the authorities." Susan indignantly said as she awkwardly hopped back on her blue bicycle and rode away.

Margaret watched until Susan was completely out of sight, before she crumbled onto the dusty ground. She wasn't going to cry, because only the weak let the opinions of others bother them; she was just so deeply exhausted. After several minutes, Margaret got up and started walking back to the house, when she spotted two recognisable small figures way out in the farmer's field behind the house.

"George! Get your butt back here!" Margaret hollered out to her son, who had wandered off a bit further than was acceptable for a toddler.

"Just a minute, mama!" George yelled back as politely as he could, not wanting to upset his mother even more.

Mary waded through the tall dry grass in the farmer's field and gave her little brother a big hug. "I've missed you so much."

George passed his sister a paper bag full of food. He had grabbed from the kitchen while his mom was talking with that lady in the front yard.

"I missed you too, Mary. Mom is mean now. I thought she would be nice now that Bad Daddy is gone, but..." George trailed off. "She's much worse."

"I'm sorry, Georgie."

"When are you coming home?"

"I don't know exactly. I made a friend, but they need my help."

"Mary! Get over here now!" Margaret shrieked as she grew closer and closer.

"I should go," Mary said as she hugged her brother tightly before turning and running away.

"Lord help me, Mary! You can't live in the woods forever!" Margaret yelled.

Mary quickly made her way across the field, before disappearing into the woods.

"At least wash your face!"

As soon as he was certain Mary was safely away from their mother, George turned to walk back home. Unknowingly, he walked through the exact spot that his stepfather was gelatinized a short week before. There were no signs of Friedrich left, save for a few fat buzzing flies.

Chapter Fourteen

Winded from her mad dash across of her family's yard and the connecting farmer's field, Mary was huffing and puffing by the time she returned to the forest. She had never run that fast before and was impressed with herself. It was a good thing that the weather was changing and clouds were rolling in, as Mary needed a break from the heat. Even though the sweat from her forehead was running into her eyes and burning something fierce, Mary was in a great mood and was looking forward to sharing her haul of snacks – mostly bread and apples – with the alien. *Do aliens like apples?* When she reached the camp though, her excitement quickly diminished.

The alien was leaning lethargically against one of the pine trees. The blue hue of its scales had faded away, leaving its skin entirely grey and slightly translucent. The alien's all too human circulatory system was visible, just under its increasingly thin grey skin. A thin milky coating was beginning to cover the alien's giant bovine-esque eyes.

"You don't look so good," Mary offered sympathetically as she crouched down next to the alien. "Here, eat this," Mary said as she passed the alien an apple.

She placed her hand on the alien's large forehead, which was cold to the touch. Mary didn't know much, or anything really, about the health of aliens, but she could tell that something was very wrong. She prayed that there was some truth to the adage about an apple a day keeping doctors away.

Maybe some rosehip tea would help? They weren't supposed to be in season yet, but Mary swore she spotted some growing along the perimeter of the forest during her run. She grabbed the bucket made of birch bark that she had made a few days earlier and walked down to the edge of the creek to retrieve some water.

While filling up the bucket, Mary caught a glimpse of her reflection in the water. Never a vain child, Mary was still taken back by how dirty her face was. She looked like a hobo! Mary frantically splashed water on her face, determined to look more like the spry nine-year-old she remembered seeing in her bedroom mirror only a week ago. Unaware of just how bad this day was going to get, Mary was startled when she spotted her rivals Lucy and Ricky making their way up the creek.

"Oh no..." Mary hurried back to the alien. "You need to hide. Now!" The alien looked at Mary sluggishly.

"Some bad kids are coming! They can't know about you!" Mary exclaimed as loudly as she could without yelling. She tried desperately to coerce the alien away from the tree that it was leaning on and into the bushes. Still about twenty yards away from Mary's camp, Lucy and Ricky were hopping from rock to rock, slowly making their way up the creek.

"It was so rude of Don to ditch us! The tree house ladder is a two-man job!" Lucy whined.

"Yeah, stupid Don…" Ricky muttered. He felt bad about insulting his friend when he wasn't around.

"You're just going to have to pull me up the ladder yourself."

"Not a problem, Luc. I'm stronger than Don, anyway," Ricky proclaimed, flexing his undeveloped arm muscles.

Lucy rolled her eyes and continued jumping between the stones. When she looked up again, Lucy noticed Mary frantically pacing around by a tree. *Was she talking to herself?* "Wait, is that Mary up ahead?"

"The little sheep girl?" Ricky offered.

Noticing that Lucy and Ricky had made their way to the camp, Mary stood nervously in front of the bushes that the alien was hiding in.

"Hi Maryyyyy…" Lucy mocked.

"Ba ba black sheep," Ricky reciprocated with a giggle.

"Hi you two. What are you doing here?" Mary said while shifting her weight from foot to foot.

"More like, what are you doing here?" Lucy asked while looking at Mary's camp judgingly.

Ricky paced around, picking up and examining Mary's belongings. He looked at the teddy bear, Mr. Purdy, and laughed. I think she lives here, Luc."

"You're even poorer than I thought!" Lucy joined in with Ricky's laughter.

"Just leave me alone," Mary spoke meekly, not wanting to further provoke the bullies. She walked towards them slowly, in an attempt to guide them away from her camp.

"But mocking you is just so much fun!" Lucy cooed.

"You fish, Mary?" Ricky asked, while examining Mary's duck taped old fishing rod.

"Give that back!" Mary yelled, lunging at Ricky trying to get her hands on her prized possession.

"Did your family run out of pet sheep to eat?" Lucy continued to mock.

"Maybe she's Catholic now?" Ricky suggested while holding the fishing rod just out of Mary's reach.

"That doesn't even make sense, Ricky," Lucy snapped.

"My grandparents only eat fish on Fridays. It's a religious thing—" Ricky tried to explain.

"No one cares," Lucy barked while grabbing the fishing rod from Ricky and snapping it in half.

Mary's heart went into her stomach. She didn't have any more duck tape to repair the rod. "Why would you do that? Why do you hate me so much for having less than you?"

Just as hot tears began to fill Mary's eyes, the alien leapt out of the bushes!

"B-behind y-you," Ricky stammered.

Lucy could only manage to let out a tiny scream.

The alien leaned over top of Mary. Her small stature only emphasized its terrifying seven-foot frame. It opened its mouth and stretched its jaw so widely that it looked as if it was going to eat one of the children's heads, and let out a few slight clicks before unleashing a deafening high pitch scream.

Click, click... EEEEEEEEEEEEE!

Ricky peed his pants immediately. Just as he noticed that Lucy had ran away, he could feel the hot urine flowing into his shoes. Both Mary and the alien continued to stare at him, until the boy sprinted away and was out of sight.

"You better run!" Mary proclaimed, before hugging the alien. The alien felt even colder than it did earlier. Mary realized she should start a fire as soon as she could, before the ominous dark clouds rolled in.

Chapter Fifteen

Still rattled by her confrontation with Susan Webb, Margaret decided to head into town to grocery shop. Although she didn't have much money, buying things always calmed her nerves. No, shopping for groceries wasn't glamourous, but she was looking forward to buying food for dinner without anyone telling her what to get, or complaining that she spent too much or bought the wrong kind of beer.

Margaret took a grocery cart out of its metal stall. Its handle was hot to the touch from sitting in the sun all morning. It was raining ever so slightly, but each raindrop evaporated instantly on the hot asphalt. Margaret waved her hands over the cart for a moment in attempt to cool it down, before lifting George into the buggy bench.

The cart's wheels squeaked and wobbled as she pushed the cart across the parking lot. *Of course, I had to grab the one with the bad wheel.* Margaret knew she could have turned around and gotten a shopping cart without a broken wheel, but her enthusiasm was already waning and she was growing increasingly eager to get this shopping trip over and done with.

Margaret felt judged as soon as she walked through the grocery store's doors. It was if she had a sixth sense. Douglas used to tell her that it was all in her head and that "People are too worried about themselves to judge you," but deep-down Margaret knew that the majority of the townspeople in Falkland did not like her. She could feel it deep in her gut.

Margaret picked up a box of cereal from the shelf, before noticing the price. "That much for cereal? It's just wheat!"

"Can I have some, mama?" George asked.

Maybe she was questioning her harsh parenting methods because of her earlier run in with Susan, or maybe she was just tired of turning everything into a fight, but Margaret shrugged and passed the box of cereal to George. He smiled happily, as he excitedly opened the Cheerios like they were a birthday present. Margaret began to feel oddly emotional. *28 is too early for menopause, right?*

Margaret turned to the other woman that she was sharing the grocery store aisle with and smirked. *See, I'm a decent mother.*

A few aisles, and a much fuller cart later, Margaret and George found themselves at the butcher section of the store. It was staffed by a grizzled old butcher who could have passed for an obese version of Friedrich, and his strapping young apprentice who was clearly new to the world of animal slaughter. The cooler was full of all sorts of cuts of meat. Beef tenderloin, rump roast, lamb shanks... She stared for a moment, unsure of what to buy for dinner. She debated asking the handsome young man for a suggestion.

Margaret was so used to cooking Friedrich's tough and often pellet riddled game, that she genuinely wasn't sure which cuts of meat were good anymore. Although she supposed that anything that the butcher sold was going to be better than what she had cooked in quite some time.

"Meat looks so gross," George piped up.

"It's not gross. You're made of meat too, you know," Margaret snapped.

She immediately regretted saying that, and not just because she hated the sounds George made when he cried. Even she knew that comparing a toddler to the meat at the butcher was probably inappropriate. After all, some of the meat on display was especially grotesque; Margaret always wondered who would willingly eat pigs' feet, outside of wartime?

The tall, dark, and handsome butcher's apprentice left his cutting board and walked into the freezer. Margaret began to feel indignant. *He must have seen me upset my son. He knows that I am a terrible mother! Maybe he hates my clothes?* Margaret never considered that he didn't even notice her, and simply went to the freezer because he needed to. *I'm so sick of pretty people judging me,* Margaret agonized internally, falling into her usual thought process.

Never one to pass up the opportunity to talk up a lone lady, Friedrich's fatter doppelganger walked up to the counter. "What can I get you, ma'am?" The butcher asked.

Still incensed by her perceived slight, Margaret decided to make a point. She leaned as close to the counter as she could get without smudging the glass and looked at the old butcher flirtatiously.

"Randolph, is it?" Margaret cooed, while reading his name tag.

"That it is."

"I'm trying to think of dinner plans for me and my son, but I'm plain bamboozled! What is your favourite cut of meat?"

A few fake laughs and several free steaks later, Margaret rolled her shopping cart up to the cashier. She placed each item on the counter, including George's partially eaten box of Cheerios, while making severe eye contact with the teenaged employee. This box of cereal was opened already. I'd like a discount."

The cashier looked at Margaret with disappointment, before removing the cereal from the total bill. Margaret was a notorious hassle to serve, and the cashier didn't want any problems. Knowing which customers were trouble was a benefit, or downside, to living in a small town. It depended which side of the cash register you were on.

Chapter Sixteen

Monday, June 23rd

Howling winds and rain had battered the forest Saturday night and all through Sunday. The tarp that Mary had strung up above her makeshift bed stayed surprisingly still, thanks to Mary's excellent knot making skills. However, it kept filling with water. Sensing that the unwell alien needed sleep more than she did, Mary kept an eye on the tarp throughout the night, standing up occasionally to dump out the growing pool that was hanging over their heads.

While things had since settled down, the storm had kept Mary awake for most of the last two nights. She was exhausted. The darkness of the forest wasn't helping, either. The forest was blanketed in heavy dark clouds, which kept out most of the sunlight. Mary needed to get to school though. She debated waking up the alien to tell it she was going, but figured that it was best to let it sleep. Mary tucked the alien under the blanket and kissed it gently on its forehead.

Once at school, Mary had the sinking realization that she hadn't completed her end of year solar system diorama project. In fact, with all the hecticness of living in the woods and trying to help the alien she hadn't even started it. She stood alone under a large oak tree in the front of the school for a moment, scrambling to think of a plan.

For the first time in her life, Mary was happy to see Lucy, Don, and Ricky approaching. It was a long shot, Mary thought, but there was no way that she was going to fail her class. Summoning all the courage that she could, Mary took a deep breath, held her head high, and walked towards her bullies with the confidence of a protagonist from one of Andrew Allan's Stage shows on CBC radio. Plus, more dark clouds were rolling in, so if Mary got teary-eyed, she figured that she could pretend it was rain.

Lucy and Ricky shrunk down as soon as they spotted Mary approaching. Don looked at them with confusion. If this was some new game that they thought up to torment Mary, he wasn't understanding it. "Hey loser," Don called out.

"Shut. Up." Lucy growled.

"What? Why? It's just Mary. Baaa—" Ricky elbowed Don in the ribs, mid sheep impression.

"Hi, Mary," Lucy said as kindly as she could.

Ricky tipped his hat, as if Mary was a dignitary.

Even though Lucy's words and Ricky's actions came across as even more sarcastic than usual, Mary appreciated that the bullies were at least trying not to upset her. It wasn't the respect that she would rather receive, but in that moment, she figured it would have to do.

"I need your help with something," Mary spoke cautiously. While her words were soft, she kept her head high.

"Do… do you want my diorama? It's yours if you want it," Lucy bargained.

"Mine too!" Ricky blurted out.

"No, I'm not going to steal your work," Mary said with apprehension.

"Then what do you want?" Lucy replied with a less polite tone. As afraid as she was of the alien, and by extension, Mary, she could only pretend to be nice for so long. Mary needed to hurry up.

"Things have been a little weird lately, as I uh, think you know. Could you put my name on your project and tell Miss Webb that we made it together?" Mary offered.

"Wait guys, I didn't think that these were group projects?" Don asked, causing Ricky to elbow him once more.

"Whatever you want, Mary. I'll tell teach that we worked on it together, but that you did most of the work," Lucy submitted.

"Thank you, Lucy. That is very nice of you."

Ricky passed Mary a pencil, which she used to etch her name alongside Lucy's on the bottom of a paper mâché sun. Don remained confused by the entire ordeal. Mary left the bullies, content, and walked into school. As soon as she made it through the front door of the schoolhouse, the ominous black clouds opened up and it began to pour.

Mary walked into Ms. Webb's classroom and took a seat. The class was full of various space-themed decorations and dioramas, including a large banner that read "Congratulations on a year well done!" which was stretched across the chalk board. Head still held high, Mary stared out of the window, concerned about the second wave of storm clouds that were coming in.

As soon as school wrapped for the year, report cards were handed out, and everyone said their goodbyes for the season, Mary sprinted out of the school and back to camp. She wished that she could have spent more time talking with Ms. Webb, but she couldn't squash a sinking feeling that was building in her stomach.

Back at camp, the alien was awake, but it had not moved from where it had slept. Mary approached it with apprehension. "I'm sorry I had to leave you. Did you get enough sleep?"

The alien looked at Mary, wearily.

"Well… I have some good news. I got my final marks from class?" Mary cleared her throat and put on an authoritative voice. "B plus! While not the same caliber of her usual projects, Mary gets bonus marks for going out of her way to help a struggling peer. Mary was a joy to teach, and I can't wait to see how she does next fall in fourth grade!" Mary giggled, and looked to the alien for approval.

The alien looked at her, sadly, and closed its eyes.

"You don't look well."

The alien groaned.

"No, you're still pretty. I mean that you look ill."

Mary examined the alien's bandages. The sites of the alien's injuries were inflamed. Mary had tried to keep the wounds as clean as she could, but only had iodine for disinfectant.

"Let's stay at my house tonight. It's getting late, so mom should be asleep by the time we get there. We'll sneak in."

And so, Mary wrapped her arm around the alien's bony torso, and propped its body up against hers. This was going to be a long walk.

Chapter Seventeen

After several exhausting hours, Mary and the alien eventually reached the Schmidt house. The journey between the forest and the house never usually took that long, but the previous day's storm had flooded patches of the farmer's field, making it nearly impossible for Mary to spot the gopher holes. Some puddles were deceptively deep because of this, and even worse, were tripping hazards. As Mary had to support the alien during the entire walk, she had to be extremely careful not to trip or to lead through any of the dangerous puddles. The alien's health was deteriorating fast; tripping and falling in the wet soggy field would have been a death sentence.

Inside the house, Margaret and her date, the old butcher Randolph, were lying in bed. Randolph's snoring made it impossible for Margaret to get much shut eye. She watched him with disgust as his fat chest, covered only by a ratty stained undershirt, went up and down with each breath. His snoring was something awful, like if someone had put mud in a blender. Maybe gravel. Margaret continued to stare at Randolph for some time before eventually realizing that sleep would not be in the cards for her this night.

Mary stood outside of her bedroom window. She was happy that her eyes had adjusted to the dark so quickly, because it was pitch black outside. At least it wasn't stormy at the moment. She paused though, stumped about how she was going to open this window without the help of her little brother. She knew that George would help if she woke him up, but really felt that it was best to leave him out of this. Suddenly, Mary had an idea.

"I'll be right back," Mary assured the alien, who was resting against the house's rough stucco exterior.

Mary quickly ran to the other side of the house and retrieved a large piece of firewood. The slivers jabbed her fingers and prickled her inner arms as she carried it. She placed it underneath of the bedroom window. It was still going to be a struggle to climb through the window, but at least now she could reach it.

"This is going to be tricky. We need to be quiet..." Mary whispered while putting her hands under the alien's feet. It didn't have toes, which Mary found interesting, as if the alien was wearing transparent shoes.

"On the count of two... One... Two!"

Mary lifted the alien through the bedroom window the best she could. She heard a thud as it landed, which wasn't reassuring, but was relieved when the alien stood up and looked back down at her. She climbed back up on the piece of wood and tried to pull herself into the house. Unfortunately, Mary's arms were strained from half-carrying the alien across of the farmer's field. And she sure as heck wasn't going to ask her declining one-handed friend to lift her up.

"Hang on, I'll be right there!" Mary half-hollered.

She wanted to be as quiet as she could, but her trepidation about bringing the alien into her mother's home was beginning to betray her air of confidence.

Mary ran around to the front of the house as quickly as she could. She nervously placed her hand on the latch of the screen door. She took a deep breath and tried to steady herself, but the combination of stress and exhaustion was making her hands shake. As slowly as she could, Mary pushed the door open.

Creeeeeeeeeeeeeeek.

Oh no. Just then the lights turned on, revealing the frightening figure of Margaret holding a baseball bat. Mary was surprised she still had that. She hadn't seen that thing since her mom pulled her out of little league last summer.

"Mary Louis! Where in Sam Hell—" Margaret screamed.

"Mom! I can explain—"

"Shush your mouth. I know what you're doing here."

"I just—" Mary stammered.

"You got cold and chickened out of camping," Margaret said, shaking her head. "I knew you didn't have it in you."

"I'm, uh, sorry."

"Just take off your dirty shoes and get to bed. We'll talk about your punishment for waking me up in the morning."

Mary slowly took off her soggy shoes. Her toes were so waterlogged that she wasn't sure they would ever dry out. Margaret winced when she saw her daughter's feet.

"Walk softly. Randolph is trying to sleep," Margaret called out once Mary was halfway down the hall.

"Who is Randolph?" Mary whispered.

"Your mom's new friend. Now hush up and get to bed."

Mary could hear whispers from outside of her bedroom door. She opened it apprehensively to find George sitting in on the floor with the alien.

"Are you real?" George asked while looking at the alien curiously.

The alien blinked slowly and deliberately, as if to assure George yes, it was real, and that this was not a dream.

"Can I touch you?"

The alien reached towards George and gently placed its non-injured hand in his. "Wow," George responded, awestruck.

"Hey George," Mary said with a hushed voice as she crouched down next to her brother.

"Mary! You're home!" George exclaimed while giving her a huge enthusiastic hug. "I want you to meet my new friend," he naively offered while gesturing to the alien.

"Yes, we've met. George, this is the friend that I was camping with. They're not doing well though, and I don't know what to do to help."

"Maybe they just need a good night's sleep? Naps make me feel better when I am sad."

"That's a good idea, Georgie."

With the help of her brother, Mary managed to lift the alien off the floor and led it towards her bed. The alien plopped down on to the springy mattress, which elicited a yell and a knock through their mother's bedroom wall. "Keep it down in there!" Margaret shouted, causing Randolph to groan and rollover in his sleep.

Mary placed her pillow underneath the alien's large head. She pulled up the knit blankets and tucked them in the best that she could. She placed another blanket over the alien's feet, which stuck out comically over the edge of the too small bed. George looked to Mary intently and asked, "Do you have Mr. Purdy with you?"

As luck would have it, Mary had packed up Mr. Purdy as well as a few of the other essential things from the camp before she left. She picked the damp teddy bear up out of her bag and passed it to George. George, in turn, gave the bear to the alien. "This will help you sleep," George spoke solemnly.

"You should go back to sleep too, Georgie. It's way past your bedtime."

"But I want to stay awake with you!"

"I know, but we've got to be careful not to wake up Mom and her new friend."

George reluctantly crawled into his bed. "I don't like Mom's new friend," George confessed as Mary tucked him in. "Why is Mama always friends with cruel people?"

"I wish I knew. Maybe we'll understand when we are adults."

Mary returned to the alien's side and watched it with concern. She placed the back of her hand on its head but was unable to tell if the alien had gotten any colder or not. She didn't know if aliens got fevers in the first place! This was all so frustrating. The already exhausted Mary started to feel those hot tears building up behind her eyes again.

"You're cold. But I don't know if this is normal. How do you feel?"

The alien made a few weak clicking noises.

Click... click....

Chapter Eighteen

Struggling to fall back to sleep after her run in with Mary, Margaret decided to wrap around Randolph, who was sleeping soundly – albeit, quite noisily – in her bed. His pockmarked nose released a snore as loud as a jet engine every time his fat chest inhaled and exhaled. No, he wasn't Margaret's type physically, or even personality-wise. But Randolph was no worse than Friedrich. At least, not that Margaret knew. And besides, he had a paying job. Margaret placed her thin but muscular arm over Randolph's chest, and placed her feet against his legs.

"Jesus, woman! What's wrong with you?! Your feet are freezing!" Randolph blurted out.

"I'm sorry—" Margaret apologized.

She honestly hadn't meant to wake him.

"Enough! Your sorries won't put me back to sleep!"

"Just close your eyes and I'm sure you'll be back to sleep in no time," Margaret offered, as sing-songy as she could.

Suddenly, Margaret and Randolph could hear crying coming from the kids' bedroom.

"What is that sound?"

"Oh, Mary came home a bit ago."

"Who's Mary?" Randolph asked, puzzled.

"My kid."

"I thought its name was Greg?"

"George is my son, the one you met. I've got a daughter, too." Margaret began to wish that she had conversed more with Randolph before inviting him over.

"You've got two kids?! When were you gonna tell me?!" Randolph said accusatorily while springing out of bed. He stood over Margaret in only his stained formerly white undershirt and briefs.

"I guess I just forgot—"

"You were trying to trick me!" Randolph shouted, while wagging his finger in Margaret's face. Maybe he was just as bad as Friedrich after all.

"I truly wasn't…" Margaret offered.

Even though he was clearly repulsive – Margaret wasn't blind – she really hoped that Randolph wouldn't leave. It was difficult enough to get her second husband to marry her.

"Well if I'm going to be with a woman with two kids, they better at least learn to be quiet and to respect that the man of the house needs his sleep!" Randolph grabbed his pair of trousers from the floor, but rather than putting them on, proceeded to pull the belt out of the loops.

"It's fine. Just lay back down and go back to sleep."

Randolph ignored Margaret, and stormed towards Mary and George's bedroom with his belt in hand. Margaret let out a tired sigh and followed him.

No longer crying, Mary was now sitting on the side of her bed. She was gently holding her portable radio next to the alien's head and was playing *Twinkle Twinkle Little Star* as quietly as the radio would allow. Just as the song reached its final verse, and the alien began to fall asleep, Randolph burst through the bedroom door, in all his half-dressed rage.

"Now listen here, missy—"

"I can explain!" Mary blurted out instinctively, before fully realizing that this man was a stranger, and clearly unhinged.

And with that, the alien sat-up and let out a terrifying scream. Despite the alien's failing health, it managed to shriek even louder than it had earlier.

"Sweet baby Jesus," Randolph murmured, while peeing in his already disgusting tighty-whities. From the other side of the bedroom, George tried as hard as he could to stay quiet and not giggle.

"What is going on?" Margaret asked in her usual inflammatory tone, while stepping in front of Randolph. As she took in the sight of the injured alien in her daughter's bed, she let out the loudest, most blood-curdling scream that Mary had ever heard. "OH MY GOD! MARY! WHAT IS THAT?!" Margaret wailed as she stared directly into the alien's eyes.

Sensing the obvious hostility, the alien dragged itself out of bed, and began to carry its weak frame towards the window. Even hunched over, its stature dwarfed everyone in the room.

Margaret and Randolph backed up and were cowering in the doorway.

"Mary, George… Get over here," Margaret whispered.

"Mom, it's fine."

"Now is not the time to argue, Mary!"

The alien feebly tried to open the bedroom window. Despite its height, there was such a fragility to its movements. The alien's struggle to open the window reminded Mary of a crane fly stuck on the wrong side of the screen door. "I'm not leaving it! We're friends!"

Attempting to retake control of the situation, while still in his soiled undergarments, Randolph stepped towards Mary with his belt in hand. "Don't you dare talk back to your mother like that."

The alien abandoned its attempt to open the window, and stepped in front of Mary protectively. It let out a low grumble that Mary hadn't heard before.

"I'm calling the police!" Margaret yelled before running away, with Randolph right behind her.

Mary turned to the alien and looked into its large brown eyes. In that moment she was so deeply afraid. She had only brought the alien home to heal, and now she had made everything worse.

"We need to get you out of here!" Mary said, while pulling the alien back towards the window.

"Should I come too?" George asked.

"Stay here, and hide under the covers," Mary pleaded. She wasn't entirely sure why she thought her brother should hide, but that sinking feeling she started having yesterday hadn't gone away.

Fortunately, it was easier to use the window as an escape than as an entrance. Both Mary and the alien landed on the ground, making two separate thuds. The soggy grass acted as a cushion. Mary wrapped her arm around the alien and propped it up once again. "Come on, let's go…" Mary said as encouragingly as she could to the alien.

The two of them moved inches at a time, slowly sinking into the muddy backyard. To make matters worse, it was starting to rain again.

"Get back here Mary! Leave that thing alone!" Margaret screamed from the doorstep of the house.

Mary looked over her shoulder and back at her mother. After several minutes, Mary and the alien had barely been able to reach the field.

"We've got to keep going. Please, just a bit further. I believe in you—" Mary pleaded with the failing alien.

As the alien collapsed onto the soggy earth, Randolph sprinted out of the house, now wrapped up in one of Margaret's floral housecoats and carrying on of Friedrich's hunting rifles, making much better time than his frame would suggest.

"Out of the way, girly," Randolph ordered, pushing Mary out of the way with the barrel of the gun.

"No! Don't hurt it! We're friends!" Mary prayed, stepping between the shotgun and the alien.

"No one is friends with a monster," Randolph said, not understanding the irony of his words. "Now move!"

"No!" Mary roared.

In that moment, half of a second slowed down to what felt like an eternity. Using its good arm, the alien pulled Mary to its side, and out of the way of the shotgun blast. The alien collapsed, gasping. Randolph had not picked up the pellet gun by mistake, as Mary was hoping he had. Having been hit just under its neck, the alien's chest was torn open from the close-range force of the blast.

"No, no, no! Please don't die," Mary pleaded while trying to stop the bleeding. Her hands looked especially small in the moment, as she tried to plug the wound in the alien's chest. "I can't lose you. You're my only friend. Please, please don't leave me here."

The alien took Mary's hands off of its chest and held them tightly in its singular fist. It let out a few soft clicks, while gesturing to a spot in the northern corner of the sky with its other arm. It looked Mary intensely in the eyes and communicated something that only she was to know, before the light faded from its large eyes.

By now, the rain had turned into a torrential downpour. Mary leaned over the alien and gave it one final hug. Covered in an awful mixture of mud and blood, Mary lunged at Randolph with all the force that her nine-year-old body could muster.

"How could you do that? I hate you! I hate you so much! I wish you were dead!" Mary screamed and wailed while kicking and punching Randolph.

Unsure of how to respond, Randolph pushed Mary off of him and tried his best to keep her at arm's length. Finally leaving the safety of the doorstep, Margaret ran over and grabbed Mary, trying her best to keep her away from Randolph.

"Let me go! You're as bad as he is!" Mary continued to yell while trying to escape her mother's grasp.

Chapter Nineteen

Thursday, July 3rd

Once again, Mary was sitting at her bedroom window. Her head in her hands, with her elbows propped up on the ledge of the windowsill. The inner parts of her arms were pink with sunburn as she hardly moved from this spot. George had begun to tease Mary that she was turning into a houseplant. Today was the third of July. Nearly two weeks had passed since the alien was shot in front of Mary. Nearly two weeks had passed since she placed her hands on its chest to stop the bleeding. Nearly two weeks had passed since Mary last looked her mother in the eyes...

While Mary admittedly didn't understand the complicated world of adult relationships, she found it disturbing that her mother was still seeing the man that had murdered Mary's best friend. At least Mary assumed that her mother was, anyway. Mary hadn't left her bedroom, except to use the washroom.

"I brought you a snack," George whispered, while sliding Mary a plate with a piece of cake.

"Thank you," Mary muttered, without shifting her gaze.

George watched his sister for a moment, before leaving.

Mary looked down at the piece of vanilla sheet cake. It was primarily white, with little bits of red and blue icing. When intact, the cake had read "Happy Dominion Day!" Mary's current piece just had "ay!" on it, which felt much more celebratory than she was currently comfortable with. While Mary hadn't attended the party, she had watched her family attend the neighbourhood's Dominion Day celebrations from afar. She poked at the cake with disinterest, before picking up the fork and taking a bite. The cake wasn't terrible, but it was starting to dry out, as it had most likely been left on the counter since the party happened two days ago.

Mary swallowed the cake. It was dry and stuck as it went down her throat. She momentarily debated leaving her room to get a glass of milk but didn't feel up to that yet. She pushed the plate of cake away and continued to stare outdoors. If Mary closed her eyes, she could imagine that the clicks of the grasshoppers were coming from the alien.

Later, as dusk was approaching, George came back into the bedroom. "Mom is mad you missed dinner." Understanding his sister's silence, George sat next to Mary and placed his head on her shoulder. Mary looked over at her little brother and placed his hand in hers.

Mary awoke in the middle of the night to find that she had fallen asleep looking out the window. She looked over at George, who was fast asleep in his bed. It made her slightly sad that he no longer needed her to tuck him in at night. She stood up and placed her bare feet on the coarsely carpeted floor, which felt like standing on a bed of nails. Apparently sitting in one spot for that long could make someone quite sore. After eventually shaking the pins and needles feeling out of her feet, Mary finally decided to leave her bedroom.

No longer caring if she woke anyone up, Mary walked down the hall. The faded pink walls of the hallway were strewn with framed old photos from happier times. Photos of a smiling Margaret holding George and Mary as babies. A drawing that Mary made when she was in kindergarten. An old family photo with Mary's late father, Douglas, holding George as a baby in the hospital. Mary wasn't sure if this picture was from when George was a newborn, or if it was from when their dad was in the hospital at the beginning of his cancer treatment. Sometimes Mary would stop and stare at these old photos. Stopping to trace the old images with her finger, as if she could still reach out and touch her father. As if the picture was a portal into happier times. Tonight though, Mary did not feel like looking at the photos.

Out of habit, Mary still caught herself dodging the squeaky spots on the floor. It wasn't because she was worried about her mother's wrath, though. at this point Mary didn't care about anything. No one could do or say anything to her that would make her feel any worse. What was her mother going to do? Yell at her for waking up Randolph again? Nothing mattered anymore.

The closer that Mary got to the kitchen, the more that she could feel the vibration of the refrigerator on her feet.

While the humming of the refrigerator was usually overpowered by daytime atmospheric sounds, conversations or more often than not someone yelling, at night the mechanical rumblings of the fridge were quite noticeable.

With only the moon lighting her path, Mary found her way into the kitchen. She opened the cupboard that was next to the fridge, grabbed a glass, and poured herself some milk. The stale cake that she had eaten earlier was most certainly digested by now, but the milk was still refreshing. As Mary finished drinking the glass of milk, she spotted the faint glow of a lit cigarette from someone sitting at the kitchen table.

"Everyone thinks that this family is a freak show," Margaret muttered.

Mary stood in place, frozen.

"While you were out having your little adventure, I was trying to keep a roof over your little brother's head. Not that you care though, you unappreciative brat." Margaret took a deep pull on the cigarette and let out a phlegmy cough. Mary remained still, hoping that if she went long enough without speaking that her Mother would get bored and leave her alone. "Do you think things have been easy for me since your father left?"

"He didn't leave, he died," Mary attested.

"Same thing."

"Dad didn't want to leave us. He was sick. I remember."

"Can't you ever just nod and smile and agree with what I am saying? Why'd you always have to be so combative?" Margaret ashed her cigarette in a coffee cup and stood up. She teetered ever so slightly as she looked down at Mary. Mary wasn't certain, but it looked like her mother had been drinking. This was especially jarring to Mary, since she knew how much her mother typically hated liquor. "Apologize to me," Margaret slurred.

Mary continued to stare back at her mother. She knew whatever she said to her was going to be misinterpreted, so she figured that it was best to remain silent. Margaret took another deep drag from the cigarette.

"I didn't want Randolph to kill your friend, you know." Margaret picked up the coffee cup off the table and mashed her cigarette into it. "We all make mistakes," Margaret muttered, as she turned and walked warily down the hallway, leaving Mary alone in the dark kitchen.

Chapter Twenty

Tuesday, July 8th

Just as she had spent every day that week, Mary was once again sitting by her bedroom window. Sometimes her gaze would wander, and she would catch herself watching other kids playing on the street. Mary wasn't watching them with any sort of jealousy or envy though; she didn't feel that she was missing out on anything by not being their friend. She mostly watched them with curiosity. Ever since Mary befriended the alien, regular life felt surreally mundane. *How can everyone act like everything is normal when there are aliens out there?* Mary would wonder. Sometimes that curiosity would shift to anger though, as she also couldn't understand how life seemed to continue as normal even though someone so important to her just died. Mary felt as if her emotions were on a pendulum.

While Mary sat quietly by the window, Margaret and Randolph would occasionally place their head against her bedroom door to listen it. They wanted to know why exactly she spent all day, every day, looking out of that damn window. The only option they didn't consider was to ask Mary how she was feeling.

"Your girl isn't right," Randolph mumbled to Margaret, with a hint of disgust in his voice.

"She's in mourning," Margaret empathized.

"Over that freak? I did her a favour."

"She's my daughter, not yours. Let me worry about this." Margaret rebutted.

"Whatever, woman." Randolph left his spot outside of Mary's room, and stomped down the hall like an oversized and unwashed petulant child. That was it. Margaret was sick of this behaviour. She was tired of people disrespecting her. She couldn't even get her own daughter to speak to her anymore, and now this lowlife that only made her relationships with her children worse was talking down to her? True, he had a good paying job, and Margaret had no idea how she would support her family without a man, but she had finally reached her breaking point.

"Don't talk to me like that," Margaret spoke with an authoritative tone that she wasn't sure if she had ever directed at a man before.

Randolph froze in his tracks. "You're certainly uppity. Where's this coming from?"

"I think you should leave."

"Make me," Randolph replied with a disgusting grin.

Margaret eyed the baseball bat that she kept sitting by the front door of the house but decided to solve things with words this time. Margaret was amazed at just how much power the words "I am going to report you for slaughtering illegally hunted animals" had over the old butcher. The contact information that the Conservation Officers gave her a few weeks earlier turned out to be surprisingly useful.

While George was mostly focused on colouring at the time and wasn't quite sure why Randolph left the house so quickly, he knew that this was good news, and had to share it with his sister. He ran down the hallway as quickly as his little legs would take him and hopped up next to Mary who was still seated at the bedroom window. George breathed deeply, to catch his breath after running there so quickly.

"Good news! Mom made her friend leave. I didn't like him," George said with a gasp. "Mary?" George lightly tapped on Mary's shoulder. She had fallen asleep. He walked over to her bed and grabbed the comforter off it. He dragged the large blanket across the room and draped it over his sister's shoulders.

Having once again missed dinner, Mary woke up from her windowsill nap long past nightfall. She breathed deeply and filled her lungs with the gentle summer night air. The sky was pitch black and strewn with stars. She noticed the blanket wrapped around her, and her little brother sleeping soundly in his own bed. In that moment, everything was quiet. Even the crickets were asleep.

Mary walked over to George's bed, and gave him a kiss on the forehead. Even though he was so young, she was grateful that George was always there for her. And then, for the first time since she lost her friend, Mary smiled.

Suddenly, Mary spotted something out of the corner of her eye. *What was that?* Mary jumped up and ran back towards the window. The remnants of a bright blue streak floated in the atmosphere for a few seconds, before fading completely. Even though she hadn't seen the ship clearly, Mary knew deep down in her gut what had happened. She ran back to George, and gently shook him awake.

"George! Psst! Georgie! Wake up!"

"What is it, Mary?" George said groggily, while rubbing his eyes.

"They're here!"

"Who's here?"

"The alien's friends! I think they've come back to look for it," Mary exclaimed before running to the window. "I need to go and tell them what happened!"

"Can I come?" George asked innocently, even though he knew what his sister would say.

"George…"

"I understand. Please come home after," George bargained.

"I will."

"Promise?"

George held up his tiny pinky finger. The two of them pinky swore, earnestly.

"I love you so much George. I've got to hurry though!"

Without hesitation, Mary grabbed her bag and hopped back out of the bedroom window.

Chapter Twenty-One

Mary landed on the ground with a thud, and as soon as her feet hit the ground, she burst into a full speed sprint across the backyard and towards the forest. While she didn't see where the flying saucer had landed, she had a hunch that the aliens would be going to the quarry to look for their fallen compatriot. Falkland was a tiny town, where else would they have wanted to go? Mary wanted to be the first to reach the spaceship; she didn't trust any adults to handle the situation as well as she could.

Sensing that something was amiss, Margaret went into Mary and George's bedroom to check on her children. Noticing that Mary's bed was empty, Margaret went up to George, who was staring out the window, entranced.

"Where the hell is your sister?" Margaret demanded, with her hands on her hips.

"She went to tell them what happened to her friend," George explained, while pointing forebodingly into the distance.

"Wait. Tell who what?"

"The spacemen, Mom!" George exclaimed, exasperatedly.

Margaret bolted out of the bedroom, leaving her young son once again abandoned by the window.

Mary ran through the forest at full speed. By now she had memorized many of the hazards along the way. She knew where certain hills started, and which rocks were loose and not reliable to climb on. While her focus was on getting the quarry as quickly as she could, Mary couldn't help but have fun running through the deep dark forest now that she was no longer afraid.

At last, Mary reached the side of the quarry. Just as she had imagined, the flying saucer had landed square in the middle of the pit. Mary watched closely, as the ship's door slowly opened. Noticing lights from police cars approaching, Mary threw caution to the wind, slid down the quarry embankment, and ran towards the ship as quickly as she could. By the time Mary got to the bottom of the slope, she spotted two aliens, nearly identical to her friend, exiting the ship.

Mary waved frantically at the aliens. They looked at one another, then to Mary, and then back to one another. *What is this weird small animal trying to signal?* With the police cars now parked along the side of the quarry, Mary knew that she had to act quickly. She kept her arms in the air, trying her best to signal that she was not a threat to the aliens.

"I knew your friend! I tried to help!"

Sensing that running towards the aliens might be seen as a threat, she tried her best to slow down and walk more benevolently. Mary moved closer and closer before, without warning, she felt a slight jolt go throughout her body. It wasn't painful, just an odd feeling. It was as if she stepped through some sort of force field and was now on the other side of it. Mary now stood almost face to face with the two aliens. Or face to waist more accurately. If Mary had to guess she would have said that they were seven to eight feet tall; just slightly taller than the alien that she had befriended. Only just over four feet tall, Mary was especially tiny next to these beings.

Understanding that this child was no danger to them, the taller of the two aliens let out a series of rapid clicks while the second placed its hand on Mary's forehead. Mary closed her eyes, and in that moment understood everything the aliens wanted her to know. There was a brief yet beautiful moment of serenity, before six uniformed members of the British Columbia Provincial Police surrounded Mary and the aliens.

"Little girl, step away from the, um, not so little green men," The lead officer called out.

"Of all the things you thought you'd say today huh, Bill?" The officer nearest to him joked under his breath.

Mary turned away from the aliens and towards the police officers, and noticed her mother standing next to the officer she assumed was in charge. "They're not here to hurt anybody. They just came to rescue their friends, who crashed here earlier," Mary called out as she watched as the crowd of officers slowly got closer and closer. "I had to tell them that one of their friends died in the crash, and that the other died because... Because of adults like you." Mary looked at her mom, who was now whispering something to the lead officer.

"Listen here, missy. This is official government business. Go back to your mother!" The lead officer commanded.

"Mary! I just want you to come home so I can bake you some cookies and give you a hug…" Margaret trailed off, realizing that Mary could clearly tell she was lying.

"Ah, who am I kidding. GET YOUR ASS BACK OVER HERE NOW, OR YOU ARE GROUNDED ALL SUMMER!" Margaret belted.

"Damn…" Several of the officers muttered to themselves.

Mary turned back towards the aliens.

"Please take me with you. I am useful. I can cook, I can clean…" Mary pleaded.

The aliens looked to one another, uneasily. The pupils in their large eyes fluctuated in size.

"You have until the count of three to step away from the ship! You don't know what these creatures are capable of. They could be dangerous!" The lead officer said, while gesturing to his team to ready their weapons.

Mary grabbed on to one of the alien's hands and looked into its understanding eyes.

"Don't leave me here."

"ONE!"

"Take me with you."

"TWO!"

"Please."

"I'm so serious, lassie," The officer called out, without a tinge of hesitation.

Just as Mary turned around and looked back at the officers, the commanding officer twisted his finger in the air, signalling his men to fire.

"THREE!"

Exactly as promised, all six officers opened fire on the aliens. Mary winced, expecting the worse to happen. She kept her eyes closed and braced herself. It was only when she couldn't hear any bullets ricocheting off the ship, that Mary opened her eyes. The force field that Mary had walked through was somehow absorbing the bullets! The aliens put their arms around Mary protectively as the three of them watched the bullets that were being fired at them seemingly disappear into thin air.

As the aliens turned to lead Mary up the ramp into their ship, the officers stopped firing. Mary wasn't sure if they were stunned by everything that they had witnessed, or if it was simply because they had run out of ammunition.

"Mary, get back here! You can't go with them!" Margaret called out as she began to run towards the ship. "I know I'm lousy sometimes, but I need you at home," Margaret confessed as she walked through the force field.

Mary wondered if her mom was going to try to board the ship. As Margaret got closer though, her mood shifted once again, offended that Mary didn't immediately turn and run into her arms. "You know what? Leave! I don't care!" Margaret screamed, while taking off her shoes.

Margaret hurled the first shoe at the side of the spaceship, the second one hit the larger of the two aliens in the back of the head. Both aliens froze in place. The alien that was hit by the shoe clapped its gangly hands together, and using some unseen force, flung both shoes back out into the crowd. Margaret seethed as the judgemental aliens continued onto the ship, ignoring her.

Once Mary and the aliens were on board, the loading ramp slowly folded back into the ship, while the door began to close. As the door closed, the officers once again opened fired on the ship, this time hitting it. The bullets bounced off the ship like hail. Mary turned and looked back at her mother through the diminishing opening in the door. The flying saucer began to glow bright blue, before jetting off into space at hyper speed.

George continued sitting at his bedroom window, staring off into the distance with his cardboard telescope. When he spotted the magnificent blue light stream across of the sky, he realized that his sister had left him behind. He knew that Mary would return one day though; she had pinky sworn.

ACKNOWLEDGMENTS

Thank you to the following amazing individuals:

Chorong Kim, for illustrating the cover;

Susan Mayo, for editing and proofreading this book;

Samantha Braconnier, for providing such encouraging and helpful feedback;

and Graeme Good for being my rock and biggest cheerleader. I love you.

ABOUT THE AUTHOR

Ashley Good is an author and independent filmmaker
from British Columbia, Canada.

She resides on Vancouver Island, where she also hosts the
Foggy Isle Film Festival, an annual macabre film showcase.

You can check out more of her work at ashleygood.ca.